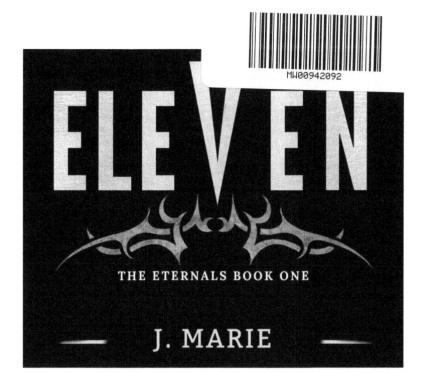

ELEVEN

THE ETERNALS BOOK ONE

J. MARIE

ELEVEN

Copyright © 2019 by J. Marie

All rights reserved.

WARNING: This book contains sexual situations, violence and other adult themes. Recommended for 18 and above.

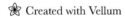 Created with Vellum

ELEVEN

I've spent my entire life being trapped and studied like the lab rat I was created to be. Tortured, prodded, abused, I dreamed of freedom, but didn't believe I would truly find it. I never thought my chance of getting away would come in the form of a sweet, little girl with secrets of her own.

ETTIE

I could hear his screams late at night when I was supposed to be sleeping. Each one of them marked me, scarring me on the inside, where no one could see…but me. I hid my secrets, knowing what I was doing could get me in trouble. I only knew that I had to help him. I loved him, even if I was too young to have him. I knew in my heart that someday he would be mine and I would be his. I helped set him free, my beautiful soldier with the smoldering brown eyes and crooked smile. But, when I needed him, he was nowhere to be found. Now, he's back, but dreams to a child are simplistic. Things are different when you're a woman and the man you're in love with, have always been in love with, holds the power to completely destroy you.

Welcome to the world of the Eternals. Supernatural beings finding their way in a world they don't belong to, yet have no choice but to live in. The only thing that might make it tolerable is one truth. Somewhere out there, every single one of them has a true mate. Now, they won't stop until they find them. Who knows? Maybe it could be you.

Prologue

She could hear him screaming. Her stomach twisted at the sound. She pulled her legs up against her chest and wrapped her arms tightly around them. Her small body rocked back and forth.

She could hear his cries. Sometimes she heard them days later. Each one marked her. Each one became a living thing inside of her. She couldn't help him. She was too little. But, one day she swore…

She would save him.

Small doesn't mean weak.
　—*Ettie*

"*They hurt you again.*"

I tilt my head to the side. Her words were there, inside of me, but it was more than that. I could feel her. I don't know how that is possible, but it was, just the same. Maybe I am going insane. It's not like that is outside the realm of possibility. After all, I've been in this small six by nine cell my entire existence. I'm not sure how old I am, time doesn't hold much meaning. But, the way that the experiments are intensifying shows that I'm becoming stronger, because I'm not being treated like the others in the room.

"*Why won't you talk to me?*"

"*You're not real. You're just another one of their tricks.*"

"*I'm real.*"

"*You would say that to convince me to believe in you,*" I reason.

I curl up on the small cot that serves as my bed. The mattress is little more than an inch thick. There's a hard, clear material that comes out of the wall it rests on. The material may look like glass, but I haven't been able to chip or break it over the years, nothing seems to penetrate it. Then again, the entire room is made of that same clear material, so maybe it was specifically formulated to be used for prison.

Eleven

And that's what it is, a prison, despite the guard always referring to it as a chamber. It sure wasn't a home, that much I am sure of. I've never had a home—just this large lab that holds these cells…chambers.

There is a series of seven chambers, built around a central area that the guard and some of the scientists work at. You can see into each chamber, nothing is hidden and because of that, I see everyone that is here. It's how I know that there are others who endure the same treatment I do—if not worse.

The chambers are soundproof, unless my captors push a small button on the door, so they can hear me talk and vice versa. I am isolated and yet surrounded by others. Somehow that makes me feel more hopeless.

I groan as I turn to my side. The pain from today's experiments is so severe that my body feels like it's throbbing. Instinctively, I know that I can't survive much longer. There's no way I can. I'm not old enough to withstand it. I do have some strength, but they keep injecting me with this medicine that keeps me weak.

I heard the scientists and guards laughing about it. I'm supposed to be the key to the perfect weapon, but they don't care if I survive. I'm just one single step toward their goal. They've been building my kind—weapons—for years and rarely had what they deem successes. I'm the closest they've come. I'm number eleven. The ten before me?

A few still live…

Almost against my will, my gaze travels to the container beside me. It's empty now. Last week, it was filled by the one they called Three. He was old, the oldest here. They had cut him open in their last experiment. Normally, Three's body healed itself, this time it didn't. Even through the chambers I could smell the man's blood.

Then again, blood is my weakness.

"It makes me sad that you don't talk to me."

Guilt hits me. She was nice to me, my only friend. She

5

talked to me all night sometimes. I don't know who she is or how she can reach me, how her voice gets inside of me. And, maybe, that is why I don't trust it—can't fully trust her.

"What if you're just another tool to hurt me? To break me?"

"I wouldn't hurt you. I like you."

"You don't know me."

"I do. I see you every night."

"I don't see you."

"You don't dream," she says and I frown, my brow creasing as I try to piece together what she's saying.

"What does dreaming have to do with it?"

"When I dream, I can go anywhere I want."

"Why would you want to come here?"

"Because that's where you are, silly. I'll always want to go where you are," she says simply.

"How do you dream?" I ask, thinking that all I ever have are nightmares, memories of torture.

"You sleep and think of something that makes you happy."

I think about it, and realize I can't dream.

"I've never been happy."

"One day, I'll make you happy," she promises, her voice growing faint as my eyes grow heavy. They had injected me with medicine after running electricity through my body and running tests on my heart. I want to stay awake to ask her more questions, but I can't.

6

2

Ettie

Excitement runs through me and I can barely hold still. My mother never lets me come to work with her. Today she had to, because my nanny was sick. I won't be here long. She just had to come in to drop off a file, but still the fact that I'm here is *everything.* I never thought it was going to happen.

My mother holds tightly to my hand as we go down the small corridor toward the main area. There are no windows, because it's an underground bunker and the only light comes from the fixtures in the ceiling. They are bright florescent bulbs and they hum so loudly the sound annoys me. I'm not scared though and I know exactly where I'm going, because I've seen all this before.

In my dreams.

I don't tell her about that though, not anymore. It makes her mad and I don't like it when she's upset.

She hurts me.

"Esther, quit fidgeting," Mother says, sternly. I didn't realize that I was moving. I immediately tighten my body to keep from betraying my excitement.

I hate the name Esther, not that I've ever told her that. I try to tell her as little as possible. Most of the time, I try to make her think I'm never around. Life is easier that way.

She scans the card she wears around her neck and the doors slide back. I keep my eyes down as we walk to the center of the room, my mother's heels clicking against the concrete floor. I know he's here, but I can't look, not yet.

"Sit here, Esther, and don't you move. You can color if you wish. I won't be long, but don't leave this spot. The last thing I need is for you to get in trouble. I had to get permission to have you with me this morning. We'll be gone as soon as I talk to my boss."

"Yes, Mother," I say softly. I'm only ever allowed to call her mother.

I take out my crayons and coloring book as my mom walks away. The guard is on his phone and ignoring me. I already have my page colored. I did that last night when Mom said I'd have to come into work with her today.

She warned me that I shouldn't give her any problems about going with her this morning because it was so early. She had no idea how happy I was. I've been wanting to come here ever since I dreamed my first dream of him…

I slide off my chair and sneak over to my friend. He's prettier in person. His hair is dark and shiny. He doesn't look up as I go over there, but that's okay. He's lying on the bed and I know it's hard for him to move.

They hurt him last night.

I hate when they do that. I hate that I can't do anything to help him. I'm too little right now, but one day…

I fold up my picture and then stand on my tip toes to reach up and hit the button so he can hear me.

"Hi," I whisper.

He jerks up off his bed and I can see even that small movement causes him pain.

"It's you!"

"Shhh...," I hush him. I look around to see if anyone is paying attention. "They'll hear."

"You're real," he says.

"I told you I was."

"I didn't believe you."

"Now, you have to. We can be friends."

"You're just a little girl," he says and I might be young, but I can hear the disappointment in his voice and it makes me frown.

"I won't always be."

"Yeah, but you can't help me."

"I will someday," I promise him.

"It will be too late."

"It won't," I argue, but he turns around, ignoring me. I slide my picture through the small opening where they give him his food. Maybe he will look at it later. "Goodbye," I whisper. I hoped he would say something back, but he doesn't. "It's rude not to talk back to someone who wants to be your friend," I instruct him. He still doesn't say anything, and I can't risk standing there any longer. I reach up and turn off the speaker. Then, I scurry back before my mother discovers I'm gone.

My friend never does turn and look at me and when we leave, he doesn't even acknowledge me then. I notice the paper is missing though, so I know he got my picture.

I hope he likes it.

3

#11

I move to the corner of the room. It's the one spot in the room that I'm not monitored constantly by cameras. I slide down against the wall, sitting on the floor. My body is too sore to move without the added support. As it is, standing back up will be hard to achieve.

I unfold the paper the little girl gave me. I still can't believe she is real. I should, considering what I am and my reality, I should be able to believe anything, but until I saw her face to face, heard her voice in person, I thought she was a figment of my imagination—someone I created because the torture had splintered my mind.

It's a picture of a princess, colored in bright blues and pink. The princess is holding hands with the prince. Below the picture, she's written two words. The first is the word us and it has an arrow drawn to the center of the prince and princess. Then it has her name.

Ettie.

"You have a pretty name."

I never have to say the words out loud. I just kind of think them and her voice is in my head. This time, though, she doesn't answer. I probably made her mad. She's listening, because I can feel my connection with her. It's frustrating that she doesn't answer, but it's no less than I deserve. I fold the paper back up and slip it under my mattress. I don't want them to discover it. I should be sleeping. I've been tortured hours upon hours. It was bad, maybe the worst yet and if the pattern holds, they will give me the next two days off and pick on one of the other captives. I'll need every spare moment I can get to rest and prepare for the next wave. I can't though. My thoughts are too chaotic. It's hard for me to believe the voice was real, even if it came from a little girl. A little girl who was here inside of my prison, and left with one of the white coats. I knew her. She wasn't the one to torture me, but she's usually present during the sessions, making notes on a clipboard that she's always packing with her.

What does that mean?

I wish I could understand. Maybe it's not important and I should just forget about it, block the little girl from my mind completely. If I'm honest, I don't really want to do that. Most of the time, she's the one bright spot to my days. Her voice even manages to lessen the pain that I'm in at the time.

"Breakfast."

My head jerks to the front of my container as the guard pushes a button and a twelve by twelve square drops down from the door itself, turning into a shelf. He places a glass down on it and it slides inside. I get up and take the glass, knowing if I don't, I won't be fed again for days. I need the nourishment if I'm going to survive.

I take the glass and the tray slides back out and doesn't stop until it seals into the door again. I memorize where the slot is—for the millionth time. I've secretly been testing it, to see if it has some kind of weakness that I can exploit. So far, I've found none, but I'm going to keep trying. I don't have a choice.

Unless I give up.

That possibility is always in my head. There's no reason for me to live. What I'm doing is existing, not living. I don't really

JORDAN MARIE

have a reason to keep going. I put the glass down on the small table by my bed.

There's no point. There's nothing for me.

"Don't give up, I need you."

The small voice flutters through my mind. Ettie.

It's silly and maybe I'm a fool. I reach over and grab the glass I was given. The coppery tang of blood slides down my throat and instantly I feel more alive.

"I'll try for you, Sunshine. I'll try."

```
┌─────────────────────────────┐
│                             │
│             4               │
│                             │
│           Ettie             │
│                             │
└─────────────────────────────┘
```

T*wo Weeks Later*

"YOU'VE BEEN QUIET."

I hear my friend, and I wipe the tears from my face with the back of my hand.

"Sorry."

"What's wrong, Sunshine?"

"My mother is mad."

"The woman you were here with?"

"Yes."

I don't want to tell him about her, I know she's part of the ones that hurts him. I've seen it in her dreams, but I'm careful never to let her know I see her dreams. She would use it. I might be little, but even I know that.

"What did you do?"

I bite on my thumbnail and try to figure out how to answer. I don't really want to.

"Ettie? Are you there?"

"I'm here."

"What happened?"

"She found out I visited you. She said I shouldn't draw 'tention to myself."

"What did she do to you?"

I can feel that he's mad at my mother. He's upset that I got in trouble. That has to mean he likes me a little, too. Now we're real friends.

"She put me in the dark."

"The dark?"

"She locks me in my closet when I'm bad. I don't like it. I'm..."

"You're what, Ettie?"

"You'll laugh."

"No I won't."

"Promise?"

"I promise."

"I'm afraid of the dark. There's bad things in the dark."

"Are you still in the closet?"

"Yeah."

"What if I promise to stay with you until she gets you out?"

"Can you?"

"They shouldn't come for me for a little bit."

"They hurt you last night?"

"No. They have a new subject they're focusing on. Number twelve."

"You're eleven."

"Yeah, I know."

"What's your real name?"

I should already know. Friends should know these things. I frown cause I feel bad I haven't asked.

"I don't guess I have one."

"What did your mother name you?" I ask, looking down at my toes because that's the only thing I can make out in the dark. I have my arms wrapped tight around my legs and my knees pulled back against my chest. I try not to take up a lot of space in here. Maybe if I don't, the monsters won't find me.

"I didn't have a mother."

"How were you born?"

"In the lab I guess."

I can sense he doesn't like talking about this.

"You need a name."

"Eleven."

"Something besides that."

"You name me."

I think about it, and smile when I think of a name.

"Max."

"Max? It's not bad. What made you think of that name?"

"It's the name of the Grinch's dog when he steals Christmas."

"I don't know what that means, but I don't want to be named after a dog."

I giggle because I can't stop myself.

"I like your laugh, Sunshine, but no dog names. Don't you know the name of a ferocious beast, like a lion or a tiger."

"Simba?"

"Uh, no." The way he says that makes me giggle.

"How about Leo?"

"Leo... that's not too horrible."

"Then you're Leo."

"I guess, I am."

I smile, and for the first time since my mother put me in the closet yesterday, I'm not scared.

Leo is with me.

```
┌─────────────────────────────────┐
│                                 │
│                5                │
│                                 │
│              Ettie              │
│                                 │
└─────────────────────────────────┘
```

F our Years Later

"LEO, ARE YOU THERE?"

I can't keep the panic out of my thoughts. It's been over a week since I've heard from him. He even missed my thirteenth birthday. I even got so desperate that I searched my mother's dreams. I still shiver when I remember those. Always before, when I witnessed the torture that Leo or one of the others endured, it wasn't my mother who performed it. She was merely a bystander, taking notes. This time, she helped hurt Leo and she enjoyed it.

"Leo, please answer me."

I'm scared they killed him this time. If they did, it will be all my fault. I should have tried sooner to search for ways to get him out. Now, I'm afraid it's too late.

"Leo, please."

I'm crying now, I can't keep from it.

"Leave me alone."

The relief I feel when I hear his stilted words is indescribable. It washes through me like a hurricane force wind, giving me relief but robbing me of air.

"Leo, you're alive."

"Barely."

"You'll get stronger, I have a—"

"No."

"Leo?"

"I'm done, Ettie. I'm tired of trying. I'm never getting out of here unless I'm dead."

"You can't, Leo! I—"

"It's over. I've refused the stuff they give me. I haven't digested anything in days."

"You have to, Leo. I finally found a way to help you."

"There's nothing you can do to help me, Ettie. You're a baby and you have no idea the hell I've been through."

"I went into my mother's dreams when I didn't hear from you."

"I don't want to talk about your mother."

He growls the words and the hate behind them drips through our connection and it feels as if it bleeds into me.

"I searched her mind."

"I thought you said that was dangerous, that she would feel you there."

"It is, but I think I disguised myself enough. I only did it briefly."

I hope he can't tell the worry I actually feel. My mother has been watching me closely since that time. I'm starting to think I wasn't careful enough.

"You're worried."

"I'm fine," I lie. *"But, I think I found a way to help you at last."*

"What is it?"

"They're developing a serum. They're close to success. They've been giving it to the test animals there at the facility."

"What kind of serum?"

"The monkeys can control objects for short periods of time."

"Objects?"

"Like, one monkey made a banana come to him."

"I don't think a banana will help me get out of this place, Ettie."

He's back to sounding helpless and our connection is growing weak. He doesn't have much strength. I need to convince him so he will take the food they give him. He needs to be strong for this. It's the only way.

"But, it might let you lift something to knock-out the guard."

"Even if I could do that, there's no way to open—"

"My mother keeps a spare keycard in the desk by the guard. You could pretend it's a banana…"

I sense his smile. It's weak, because he is, but I sense it and that means everything.

"I appreciate this, Ettie, but it's useless. There's no way I can get my hands on the serum to take it and even if I did, what if it didn't have the same effects on me as it did on the animals?"

"There's a risk, but you have to do something, Leo."

"Why? What's the point?"

"Because…"

"Tell me, Ettie."

"They're going to kill you at the end of the month. They've already created Number Thirteen and they've deemed at the end of the month she can go into the containment area. She's going to take your place."

"It's okay, Ettie."

He can sense my sadness, my pain at the thought of him dying. There's no way I can keep it from him. I might only be thirteen, but I've loved Leo my entire life. He's the only true friend and family I've had. While all my friends at school are talking about the cute boys, the only face I've ever had in my thoughts was Leo.

Always Leo.

He'll never be mine, and to him I'll always be a little girl. But maybe, if I can help him get his freedom, he'll be happy someday and that's enough.

6

Leo

It took two months. Two months in which I was quietly going insane. Ettie had told me everything from where the serum was and how I could use it to get free. But, what she didn't know, and I had to learn through trial and error, was exactly how to get to the serum.

In the end, that choice was taken out of my hands. Ettie's mother hadn't liked me looking at the chimps while she had me dissected. She was studying how I didn't die, despite stopping my heart from beating. The fact I wasn't suffering enough pushed her over the edge.

"You want to see what's so interesting about being a monkey? I'll start treating you like one."

"Dr. Carson, I don't think you're supposed to do that."

"I am the one in charge here. Besides, what is he going to do? We have him contained twenty-four hours a day. He can't even use the bathroom without us knowing about it. This will speed up our trials and in turn, that will make Draven happy."

"If you're sure," the lab assistant says.

I'm lying helpless, as she grabs a large needle, with glowing red liquid inside of it. I can do nothing but watch as she primes the needle and a little bit squirts out the top and onto my body. There's so much blood oozing out of me that I can't tell where it lands.

I'm on some kind of pump that constantly sends blood back into my body. The only problem is, it never sends as much back as I lose, leaving me weak.

She releases the needle into my neck, directly into the jugular. At the same time, she stops the pump and puts a clamp on my severed aorta. The pain is excruciating, the burn from the needle dim in comparison. The agony from it all is so bad that I black out, unable to fight it any longer.

I don't know how long I stay out. It could have been just a few moments, or it could have been hours. There's no way of knowing, and honestly time is relative in here anyway.

When I wake, Dr. Carson is standing over me with a dark smile on her face.

If ever there was a woman in need of death, it is her.

"I thought I had finally found something to kill you," she says, her voice matter of fact and without emotion. "The fact that you didn't leaves me kind of sad," she adds. Her voice gets kind of melancholy on the word sad, proving how sadistic she is. "Right now, the only thing I can find that will do the job, is draining you dry of blood. Which, I mean, I could do at any time. There's no point in keeping you alive, except for research. The fact you bleed out so easily makes you unreliable in battle. That upsets Draven, and makes you very expendable right now. For years I've wanted you dead. I know that you somehow lured my daughter to your cell, drawing her to Draven's attention. For that alone, you deserve to die."

She leaves the cell after that. I'm so weak that I can't even raise my head, so I lay there with the world spinning around me. I don't know if the dizziness is from the injection or the pain. At this point, I don't really care what the injection does to me. If I die, at least my hell will be over.

"Don't die, Leo. I need you."

Eleven

Ettie's voice comes slipping through my mind just as my eyes close. I've grown to love and hate her voice in the same fervor. I don't respond to her, I don't have the energy. But, for now, she will win.

I'll live at least for another day.

Ettie

F *ive Days Later*

"HELLO, ESTHER."

I jump. I can't keep from it. I'm thirteen. In all of those years, I've spent minimal time with my mother. I've never even seen my father. I don't know who he is. But, in all that time, the only time I've spent with my mother is because Amelia—my nanny—is sick or on a family trip. She lives with us, but every now and then she travels back to Georgia to see her family. Still, whenever she goes on those trips, she takes me with her. So, to come home from school, get out of the car once Clive, my mother's chauffeur, opens the door, to find my mother standing there staring down at me...*is frightening.* Her dark black hair is pulled severely to the back of her neck. Her pale face is tight with anger and she's wearing a black wool dress. The neck of the dress is a turtleneck, it has long sleeves, and is tight to her body, with a shiny black leather belt at the waist. She has black rimmed glasses and these shoes that are shiny black with impossibly high heels. She should be pretty, despite the harsh, austere dress and hairstyle, but there is nothing pretty about my mother —perhaps because the ugliness inside of her bleeds through the outside.

"Mot…. Mother," I stutter, the words so bitter on my tongue that I can taste them. My voice is full of fear.

"I warned you, didn't I, Esther?"

"I'm sorry?" I ask, my mouth going dry, my voice hoarse. I feel a tremble of fear going through me. I don't know what's going on, but I know whatever it is will be bad.

"Not yet you aren't, but you will be," she promises, her voice dripping with barely controlled anger and coldness. The coldness in her tone is so wintery that I chill just from the sound. This is the monster that my mother keeps hidden. The monster that she turns into when she is experimenting on Leo or the others. This is the monster that I fear when I'm locked in the closet.

"Mother, I don't understand."

"I warned you what would happen if you tried to explore my mind, Esther."

Panic hits me. I thought I had covered my tracks. I thought that I had managed to get information for Leo without my mother knowing. It's clear that I was wrong.

So wrong.

"But, I didn't," I lie, but even I hear the betraying guilt mangled in with fear that resonates in my tone. I take a step back, but hands slap down against each of my shoulders, holding me in place with their bruising force. I look up to see Clive looming over me, holding me and not letting me escape. My gaze darts from him to my mother, my heart beating out of control. Slowly she takes her belt loose, her cold brown eyes looking at me with hate.

"Take her to my lab, Clive. Secure her to the table."

"Yes, Ma'am," Clive responds, his voice so calm and matter-of-fact that my fear doubles.

"Please, Mother, don't do this. I didn't do anything. I didn't."

"Because of you, Number Eleven escaped today, Esther. You've put the entire project in jeopardy and Draven is very unhappy with me. I warned you not to cross me. Now, I will give you a lesson that you will never forget."

I shake my head back and forth. I scream, as Clive lifts me up in his arms, hoisting me over his shoulder. I kick and scream, but it doesn't do any good. Clive takes me inside the house, the sound of the front door shutting and my mother's heels clicking on the tile floor will probably haunt me for the rest of my life.

Everything blurs as tears burn my eyes. Most parents have rec rooms in their basement, my mother has a lab. Clive puts me on the cold metal table, my stomach down, my face pressed into the icy table, my sobs muffled as he holds me down. Then, his hand wraps around my wrist and secures me in the metal restraint attached to the base of the exam table above my head. He gets my legs secured to the end of the table, as well as my other hand, and he does all of that as if I'm not kicking and fighting him with every breath. I scream as I feel cold metal slide against the back of my thighs. It takes me a bit to realize what is happening. Then, it dawns on me that she is cutting my school uniform from my body.

"Mother, please. Please don't do this. I promise to be good. I promise," I beg, panic moving through me so deeply that it makes talking difficult. Fear is taking my breath away, causing my heart to rage against my chest, beating so hard it hurts.

She ignores me and my clothes—now ruined—are ripped the rest of the way from my body, the torn fabric under me bunching up as I flail around, trying to jerk my body free. But, it's a foolish attempt. There's no escape for me.

I cry out when I feel my mother's belt slap down against my skin without warning.

"First, I'll teach you a lesson so that you will remember to never cross me again. Then, I'm going to implant this handy little chip into your brain that will keep you from exploring any minds ever again."

"Mother," I cry, my body shaking as the belt cracks down against my tender skin again.

"You won't be able to contact Number Eleven again, and you will learn what you should have known."

"Mother," I whimper again, as the belt comes down with such viciousness, again and again, that the pain is like a red-hot heat that sears my skin.

"You are inconsequential to everyone, Esther. No one wants you," she says, right before she cracks the leather belt against my skin again—but, this time it's different. This time the buckle cuts into my flesh.

I close my eyes, the tears falling, the pain so intense that I wonder if I will die from it.

"Leo..." I reach out to talk to him. *"Help me."*

"I can't," he says, and those two words might hurt worse than the belt clawing into my back. Mother is right.

I don't matter to anyone.

```
┌─────────────────────────────────────┐
│                                       │
│                  8                    │
│                                       │
│                 Leo                   │
│                                       │
└─────────────────────────────────────┘
```

I was made not to die. Still, I almost did. I knew escaping would be next to impossible. I managed to unlock not only my cell—cage, really—but at least seven others before the guard noticed. The alarm sounded and the rest was a blur. Somehow through it all, myself and four others managed to escape. I also managed to almost die.

Bullet wounds may not kill me, but it does take a bit for my body to repair and to expel the metal from my body. But before we made it to the tunnel that led to the outside, the guards began using different ammunition—bullets that seemed to explode in my body and tear through me, the damage catastrophic. I would have died, if Number Seven hadn't thrown me over his back and packed me the rest of the way. His speed was so much faster than mine. He ran for miles, and even then, I thought I was going to die.

We're held up in the mountains somewhere now. *Caves.* We're in caves. I'm weak as water, but my body is slowly healing. Seven somehow managed to leave and come back carrying bags of blood. I don't know where he got them, but I am thankful.

I grab one, my hands so fucking weak that Seven has to hold my head up and put the blood to my lips just so I can drink it.

As soon as it hits my system, I can feel it warm me. I was so cold and I don't think I realized it until right now. Immediately it starts speeding up my healing process, but that is agony. Pain races through me as torn ligaments and muscle begin to pull and seal from the holes left by the bullets.

I cry out. I hate it, especially with the others around me, but I can't keep from it. The pain is agony. Somewhere in the middle of it, I hear Ettie's voice. Even through my pain I can feel her panic and it claws at me.

"Leo."

She calls out just as it feels like someone is sticking a heated blade through my gut. The pain is so intense that I feel like I might pass out. I don't, barely managing to hold on, but my body is shaking from the pain.

"Do you think he will live?" I hear Seven asking. He's talking to the one called Four. I don't know him. He seems colder than the rest of us, angrier—then again, he's withstood this punishment longer than the rest of us.

"He was pretty far gone. If he withstands the healing, he should," Four says, his tone even and matter-of-fact. There's no trace of emotion in him, but I suppose there's no reason there should be.

"Leo, help me," Ettie begs and I feel this intense surge of pain beginning to bloom in my chest. It's suffocating me and my vision waivers even more. I know I won't be able to keep from passing out now. I know I'm going to succumb. I fight through it to respond, but I feel my consciousness begin to slip.

"I can't," I manage to tell her, hating that she's scared, but I'm fading. If I survive, I'll talk to her while her evil bitch of a mother has her in the closet. That has to be what it is. She gets so scared when she's locked in there. Someday, I'm going to take great pleasure in killing that bitch and I'll make it extra painful, just for Ettie.

On that vow, I allow my body to go lax, shut my eyes and let the darkness come.

"Freedom isn't exactly what I imagined."

--Leo

```
┌──────────────────────────────┐
│                              │
│             9                │
│                              │
│           Ettie              │
│                              │
└──────────────────────────────┘
```

F ive Years Later

IT'S MY BIRTHDAY. That's not why I'm nervous. I'm nervous because after five years of being and doing exactly who and what my mother demanded, I'm breaking free.

Or at least I'm going to try.

I've wanted to long before now, but I've been kept under lock and key. My mother barely let me out of her sight and when she did, Clive was always with me. There hasn't been an opportunity, not one. I've been trying to squirrel money away, which isn't easy. My mother doesn't give me money and refuses to let me work after school. I've accumulated some money over the years by finding change in the laundry, doing chores for Amelia and that kind of thing. There's not much of it, however. In five years, I've managed to squirrel away two hundred dollars. That definitely won't take me far, but it will have to work. I start college next week, but Mother is not allowing me to attend a university. Instead, I am to complete online courses.

I'm a prisoner, as much, if not more so, than Leo was. The only difference is the form of torture Mother uses. Mine doesn't involve pain so much anymore. She indeed taught me a lesson I'll never forget five years ago. I go out of my way to keep my mother happy now. I've done it while plotting my escape and waiting until I could chance escaping. I might have lied. There might have been small windows in the last five years that I could have found a way to leave, but I didn't because I was scared. If I failed, Mother would kill me. Now, I don't have a choice. I heard her on the phone last night. She plans on moving me to the facility where she works full time, now that I'm eighteen. I don't know why she waited until I was of age. I couldn't tell you, my mother's mind is scary. I just know that I heard her say that Draven had given her permission to keep me at the laboratory full time. I don't have a lot of memories of the lab and the few times I've been there, but I remember Leo and the pain he endured, the bleakness in his eyes and something else. Leo was good. At least, I thought he was and I still believe it…*even though he deserted me*. Still, there were evil men in here, too. I felt it coming off of them in waves. I don't want to go there and I know that it will be a million times harder to escape from there than it will be here at home. Here, my mother leaves me to my own devices—at least most of the time. For instance, tonight she informed me that she will be at Draven's home for a business dinner. I've only met Draven twice and both times it was infinitely clear that he doesn't like children. The last time I saw him I was ten. I really hope I never see him again. I can remember that all I felt coming from him was coldness. There was no emotion other than that. It was terrifying.

Tonight I'll be left with only Amelia and Clive. I'm praying that if I escape, Amelia doesn't get in trouble. I kind of hope Clive does, and I don't care what that says about me.

I'm not prepared for my door to open and soft light to filter in.

"You're doing it, aren't you, Ettie?" Amelia asks, and I jump because I'm sneaking and putting things in my backpack...*and I'm doing it in my closet.*

I can't be sure that Mother doesn't have my room monitored. She has cameras everywhere. The one place I figure she won't have a camera is my closet. It's so small and there's no light. She also knows I'm terrified of the dark and afraid to go in my closet. I've built up my courage enough to go in there for five minutes at a time and each time I pack something else into my backpack. I don't do longer than that, because if she is monitoring me, I'm afraid she'll wonder what I'm doing. I also only do it twice a day, in case she gets curious and thinks she needs to investigate.

"I...I don't know what you mean," I whisper nervously, clutching my backpack to me and turning around. I'd try to keep the panic off of my face, but I'm pretty sure that's not possible.

"You're escaping," she says, softly.

I try to look over her shoulder, fully expecting to see Clive there. He's not, we are totally alone, but Amelia is blocking my way out of the closet.

"I...what do you mean?"

"It's okay, Ettie. Your mother can't hear and I'm blocking the camera."

"You know?" I ask, afraid to ask anything else and even though I love Amelia, I'm scared to trust her.

"Why do you think I've worked for that monster this long, Sweet Girl? I'm going to slip something in the dinner that I prepare tonight. I'll make sure that Clive eats and then I will even take some, too, just so it doesn't look suspicious."

My heart pounds hard with what Amelia is telling me and what it could mean. Suddenly, that small spark of hope that I've tried to keep a handle on explodes to life.

"You could still get in trouble," I warn her of what truly is my worst fear. I'm not sure I could live with myself if Amelia got hurt because of me.

"Don't you worry about me. I'm a tough old broad. I can handle myself. You just get free, my baby, and when you do, you run hard and fast. Don't stop for anything."

"I won't," I vow.

She reaches into the pocket of the apron she always wears and takes out a worn white envelope. "I expect you will be needing this," she says, handing it to me. I open it with shaking hands, my heart still hammering so hard that the blood is rushing in my ears. Inside there is money. It's all small bills — ones, fives, and tens. I do a quick count and realize there's over two thousand dollars there.

"Amelia, I can't…," I immediately reach out to give it back to her, but she caps her hand over mine and refuses it.

"It's not a lot, but I've been saving from the time you were thirteen and I had to doctor you. I thought the damn fool had killed you," she whispers and anguish moves over her face. I close my eyes, not truly wanting to remember the pain of my recovery, because some of the cuts of the belt got infected. It was painful and a long healing process, made worse because my mother refused to get me medical care. If not for Amelia, I might have died.

"Still, you need this money. I will be okay," I tell her and I will. I don't know how, but I know that no matter what happens, it will be better than staying here with my mother.

"Take it and set an old woman's mind at ease," she says and when I look in her eyes I give her a tight, sad smile.

"I love you, Amelia. I'm going to miss you."

"I love you, too, Esther. Now hurry and get out of there. Make sure your backpack is packed and ready for you to grab. We have two hours until dinner."

I nod my answer, as she backs away. I slip the envelope down the front compartment of my backpack, then I walk to my bed, holding it. I fish out a pen and pretend I'm filling out the forms for the online courses that my mother left on my desk this morning before she left. My gaze moves up to the clock and I watch the hand slowly move.

It's going to be a long two hours...

10

Leo

"Did we get the bunker rooms finished today?" I ask Seven.

It has taken five years of pooling together our abilities, manipulating the system and some plain old robbery to get our bank account built up. We still have a lot to do, and more to obtain, but we're stronger than we ever imagined we would be at this point. Perhaps we should feel guilty over our methods, but it's not like we were left with choices. A government agency created us, used as disposable human Guinea pigs, and planned on slaughtering us. The way we figure it, they owe us all we are taking and more.

"Yes, although the plumbing has a problem. Not sure what it is, but I think Four said it had to do with a delay on the concrete order and one of the shipments we've been expecting. It should be completed this week, however."

"That's good. Now if we had a way to know what Draven and his whore are up to," I mutter, rubbing the back of my neck. It's been five years since I've been able to talk to Ettie. I try, but when I reach out there's no connection...*nothing*. It's the oddest thing, but without being able to talk with her leaves me feeling empty.

"I don't give a fuck as long as he stays away from us," Seven

JORDAN MARIE

says, and that's the feeling that most of us have. I can't help but wonder how many others of us are trapped now. Maybe I shouldn't…but I do.

We learned after our escape that Draven's facility was in the Blue Ridge Mountains in West Virginia. We ran all the way to Montana to get away, covering our tracks as we went. It's not been easy, not by a longshot. There have been issues between us. We've all been bred to be the alpha—a war dog, if you will. We seem to butt heads coming and going because of that.

Still, for the most part, things have settled down and we have a council of three. The oldest is Four, we all look to him for guidance, so he's kind of the unofficial leader. Six and Ten make up the rest of the council. Six was elected because he and Eight seem to be different than the rest of us and Eight has no desire to serve on the council. Ten was placed in the interest that those of us who are younger have a voice, too. Maybe it is because I am so young, I have no problem going along with the vote. I only wanted my freedom, but now that I'm here…it still feels… *lacking*.

"Have you heard from the girl?" Seven asks and I frown as I feel the uneasiness that blooms in the pit of my stomach anytime I think of Ettie.

"Not at all. Not since that first night," I respond, regret thick in my words.

"She's probably dead," he says, his words stoic, not one ounce of emotion in them.

"No," I deny, honestly not having any idea, but unable to imagine the light that was in Ettie gone forever.

"You had to know they would blame the child for our escape. You said yourself that she was worried her mother would discover the way she could sift through people's brains."

"I know, but, she's her daughter…," I defend lamely.

"That bitch has no feelings. She took joy in the pain she caused. If you think that for one minute she would even blink at killing a daughter she thought betrayed her, you're insane. She would in a heartbeat."

"You're right," I respond quietly, the reality of his words bringing a strange pain that I haven't really felt before.

"And if she didn't kill the girl, she probably wishes she was dead."

"Why would you say that?" I ask, shock on my face, because I never imagined that in the last five years.

"Because they're probably taking their time dissecting her brain, trying to figure out how she does what she does."

His words bring renewed fear. Can I remain here, when there's a chance that Ettie is being punished and tortured because of me?

The answer is no. I owe Ettie. I have to go back and see if she is still alive. I have to try and rescue her...

Even if it means that I might get captured again myself.

Ettie

I look outside the window. It's dark and there's only one customer here, but I keep expecting to see signs that I've been discovered. It seems like no matter where I go, my mother or her goons are there quickly. It's been two months and I've made it to Tennessee. I've been here almost a week now and I've not seen my mother yet, but I know she'll show.

I'm not stupid. I am almost sure that the implant they put in me, to block my ability, is how they are tracking me. I just don't know what to do about it. I can't very well take it out myself and going to a hospital to demand it done is impossible. If I do that, I might as well hand myself over to my mother. I don't know what to do and I'm starting to feel like it's hopeless.

I wipe off one of the tables at my station, pulling my gaze away from the window—at least for a minute. I'm waitressing in a small diner just on the outside of Cherokee. It's on the border of North Carolina and Tennessee. We don't get a lot of traffic, most aiming for the tourist attraction that is Gatlinburg or the casino on the other side of the border. I picked here because I figured it would be easier to stay hidden. I even halfway hoped the mountains might block whatever signal this thing in my head delivers. Maybe it has. I've never been anywhere for a full week before. That also means that money is starting to be very thin. I've stretched it like crazy, living in shelters when I could and living off ramen, or soup kitchens, whenever possible. It's not great and I'm losing weight, but I prefer the way I'm living to being around my mother. There's not even a comparison.

"I'm going to close early, Esther. Doesn't seem like we're going to get much traffic tonight. If you want you can start cleaning the kitchen. I'll watch the front and lock the doors at ten," Joe says.

My gaze automatically goes to the clock above the window. Ten minutes. He knows we aren't going to get any more customers—we never do. He just wants me to clean the kitchen so he doesn't have to. He is also the cook and he's doesn't bother being neat either. The kitchen is usually a mess of grease, burnt food, and dirty dishes. I hate cleaning it, but I don't argue. He pays me cash and I have to have it—even if there's not very much of it.

"Sure thing, Joe," I mutter, walking back behind the counter and then into the door that leads to the kitchen. I want to cry when I get there, because the kitchen is in worse shape tonight than it has ever been since I started. Admittedly, this is just my fifth night, but it's so bad that I kind of want to walk out without claiming my thirty bucks. That's what I'm paid, by the way. I get thirty dollars for a ten-hour shift, and well, from the looks of this kitchen, tonight might be an eleven-hour shift.

Eleven.

I sigh a forlorn sound filled with sadness for the memories I can never forget. How it's possible to miss someone when you haven't heard from them in five years, I don't understand. I just know that I do. It's silly. He's probably enjoying his freedom, living a good life and maybe even married now. He didn't have a chip blocking his powers. My mother wanted to know what his powers were, they fed them in their quest to build the perfect soldier. So, chances are he got away much easier than I am managing. I was so stupid. I wanted to be the girl in his life—

even before I knew what that meant. At sixteen, I knew and I still wanted to be that woman. I never thought that when I needed him the most he would abandon me. I should have, but I wasn't only stupid, I was naïve.

I spend the next thirty minutes cleaning the kitchen. All that's left is the grill and taking the trash out. I stare at the grill, dreading that more than I could ever put into words. Lugging two large garbage bags to the dumpster out back seems a much better prospect. I grab the trash, one in each hand and then pull it to the door. I set them down long enough to unlock the heavy door. A small scream escapes when I see a man standing on the other side, gun in his hand.

"Ettie?"

It takes me a minute to realize I'm staring at Leo. It's not that he's changed, it's just he scared me that much. Once reality sets in, I can do nothing but stare.

Leo is here. Leo is standing right in front of me. After all this time, the only thing I can think is that this can't mean anything good…

12

Leo

It has been a little over five years, but I wasn't prepared for the changes. I know it's Ettie standing in front of me, but she no longer looks like the sweet little kid with dark curls and soulful brown eyes. She's...grown up, her body filled out, her curls still there, but softer somehow, and her hair longer. Her eyes are still the same, but even more beautiful—despite the shadows under them. I look at her and I can feel my body react. I try to squash the desire rising up inside of me. It seems wrong. This is Ettie. I can feel my teeth trying to elongate and make fangs. That's only happened two times before. Once when I was injured and required so much blood to bring me back from the brink of death, and then again when I decided to try surviving without the blood and eating regular food like Six and Eight do. All of us tried it, but none could survive. We just became weaker and weaker. Six and Eight might have been made in the same lab, but they're not the same.

I run my tongue against the fangs, shock moving through me, but that's because my gaze is zeroed in on Ettie's neck, specifically the pulsating vein that seems to pump before my very eyes. At the same time my cock widens, elongates and I can feel...hunger, but not for food.

I feel hunger for Ettie. All of us know what desire is. We read, watch television, so we've learned quite a bit since the day we gained our freedom. None of us have felt desire though. None of us have seen a woman that we wanted. We assumed that it was because we weren't normal, weren't like the human population. All of these feelings I'm having for Ettie now are bombarding me, making themselves known with a swiftness that steals my breath.

"Leo?"

My desire only grows with the sound of her voice. How can something sound so sweet, so lyrical? The melody seems to wrap around my dick, making my balls hurt because the craving for her is so strong.

What is going on?

"You've changed," I respond, clearing my throat, withdrawing my gun and putting it in a holster at my side.

"Leo, what are you doing here?" she asks, sounding panicked.

"I'm here for you. We must hurry."

"For me? But why?" she asks, stepping away from me, almost as if she's scared of me. I breathe heavy through my nose, barely containing a snarl. I don't like the idea that she could be afraid of me at all. I take a step closer, my gaze still returning to the vein in her neck, no matter how much I try to look elsewhere.

"Ettie—"

Her name comes out little better than a growl, because I'm beating down the urge to grab her and pull her into my body and kiss her…taste her…*drink from her.* I've never done that… never. Always when I must eat, it is from bags we've stolen from a local blood bank or a hospital. For the first time in my life, I want to taste it live…but only from Ettie.

What is wrong with me?

I jerk, dragging my mind back to what is going on around

us. I don't get to finish saying anything but Ettie's name, the sound of glass shattering in the other room can be heard.

"What…" Ettie turns away from me and that leaves a bitterness in me, too, but I shake it off. Now is not the time to try and decipher the feelings that Ettie is pulling out of me.

I grab her, and pull her down so that she can't be seen through the pass-through window above the counter—where I assume orders ready for serving are delivered.

"Keep down," I hiss. Moving stealthily, I move us toward the door. I open it just a little. Enough to see that it's LaDawna's— Ettie's mother's—goons. The owner has a rifle drawn and he's got a phone in his hand, but he's not going to live long enough to make a call. "Let's go," I order coldly, all but pulling Ettie with me back the way I came, keeping us low so that the men in the front room don't see us.

"But, Joe," she whispers, fear and pain in her voice.

"Will be dead," I respond, not looking at her. Just as I get the door opened and pull her outside, we hear gunfire. I don't need to look to know that the man Ettie was worried about is already dead. I can smell the blood. I turn the lock on the backdoor and close it, hoping if they think the door is locked that Ettie has either already left for the day or is somewhere else in the diner.

We get outside and Ettie tries to fight me, wanting to go back to check on her friend. I don't let her, instead I pick her up and swiftly, using a burst of the powers that I have, carry her to my car which is waiting down the street about a block from the diner. I'm thankful that it's not across from the diner or in front of it. Hopefully, we get away before that bitch's men pick up our trail.

"We have to go back and help Joe," I plead, looking out the back window of Leo's Mustang as it pulls out of the parking space.

"It's too late for Joe. Buckle your seatbelt, I'm going to see if I can put some distance between them and us," Leo orders and I automatically do it.

"It won't work."

"Trust me, it will," he replies and he's so confident, that I almost hate to burst his bubble. I know what I have to say to him next will send him away—which is for the best. I need to remember that Leo is just another person that let me down. Even as I think about it, I know I'm probably being unfair. He was just saving himself. It doesn't change things though. There's no going back. I rub the back of my shoulder at the memories that move through me, then I shake them off. I look over at Leo. He hasn't changed much in five years. His soft brown hair still has a hint of a wave to it. I'm not sure I remembered how long and thick his eyelashes are. I'd kill for lashes like that. His body is firmer and maybe I've forgotten, but he seems more muscular and broader. He's wearing all black, including a turtle neck sweater that is definitely stretching across his torso and accenting his muscles. My gaze moves to his hands, large, rough hands that have ink tattooed on them that I can see, even in the darkness.

"Fuck," he hisses, his dark voice growling out in a way that sends shivers over my body—and not the kind that you get when you're cold.

"What is it?" I ask, my eyes studying the tight lines on his face and the white-knuckled grip he has on the steering wheel.

"They're right behind us. I can't figure out how. We left the diner before them and were in the car before they even came out and yet, here they are, and I didn't take the main road. It should have been good enough to lose them at least for a little while."

I look over my shoulder seeing the lights of the car behind us shining bright and you can tell from the movement that the driver is handling the vehicle erratically. A sick feeling hits me in the pit of my stomach.

"You have to let me out," I tell him quietly.

"You're crazy. They'd grab you within seconds. I've been searching for you for over a month. LaDawna's men have been chomping at the bit to get their hands on you," Leo argues. I already knew that my mother's henchmen have been trying to find me, of course. Somehow hearing it out loud makes everything worse.

"I'm serious, Leo. You have to let me go. They won't stop and there's no way you'll be able to get away from them if you don't."

"I've hidden from them for over five years, Ettie. I'm pretty sure I can handle myself now," he says so confidently that it also sets me at ease—but then, I know something that he doesn't.

"Leo, you won't get away from them. They can track me. You have to let me go."

"I'll cover our tracks so they can't find—"

"It won't work," I insist again, my voice near panic. Leo got his freedom, just trying to have me with him will jeopardize that.

I might survive if my mother gets me back, but she will kill Leo. I don't even have to guess about that. She wants him dead.

"Let me worry about this, Ettie. Just hold it together and keep quiet long enough for me to lose these jokers," he barks, clearly upset. Telling me to keep quiet should piss me off, and it does annoy me. I also take a moment to admire the husky timbre in his voice. I've always been fascinated with Leo. Apparently, time apart and growing up hasn't changed that.

It might have made it worse.

"They're tracking a chip my mother implanted in my head, Leo. You won't be able to lose them, because they will always find me. You have to let me out of here. It's the only way you'll be safe."

"She put something in your head?" he asks, daring to take his eyes off the road to look at me.

"My neck really, but yes. Do you see now? You have to let me out of this car."

"That's not happening. If they can track you, we'll just have to make sure they're all dead."

I blink at his words and the easy, matter-of-fact way he delivers them.

Before I can question them, Leo thrusts his foot down on the gas pedal, the car immediately responds, and I'm too busy to do anything but hold on and fear that I'm going to lose my life in a fiery car crash.

I twist my neck, popping it, smiling at the glow of fire in my rearview mirror.

"I can't believe that just happened," Ettie says, sounding awestruck. "How did that even happen?" she asks. I glance over at her and she's looking over her shoulder at the carnage. The orange of the fire's glow seems to shine in the car just a little, but enough to shine on her dark hair. I'm having trouble reconciling in my mind how the cute girl I remember could have grown into such a beautiful woman. It's even harder to understand why my body seems to be reacting to her, when it has refused any other woman I've ever come in contact with.

"The cars crashing? They took the turn too fast and don't have my reflexes. I guess that's something I can thank your mother and Draven for," I mutter.

"But they exploded. I've never seen a car do that," she says.

"They had some help."

"Help?"

"Seven and I planted explosives under their cars before I ran to the alley."

"How did you manage that without them seeing you?"

"We have some talents," I respond, with a shrug. "There's a hotel up on the right that's where I'm to pick Seven up at."

"You need to let me out here."

"Not happening."

"It has to. Just because you got rid of my mother's men this time, it doesn't mean anything. There will be more behind them. They won't stop coming after me, and this thing inside of me will lead them right to me, every single time."

I study her for a minute, the earnestness on her face, the panic that has receded, but still evident in her eyes. "How long have you been running?" I ask, trying to put all the pieces together that are moving around in my head.

"Not long enough," she mumbles, avoiding my gaze and looking out the window.

"How long?"

"A couple of months. Long enough to know that I'm not ever going to be free. They'll succeed in taking me back someday."

"If you feel that way, then why are you running at all?" I ask, confused.

"Because when she captures me, she will kill me," Ettie says softly, but with such surety that it could chill your blood.

"You're her daughter," I try to argue, but even I know my response sounds hollow.

"You know my mother as well as anyone. She wouldn't let the fact that we share DNA get in her way."

We're silent for a bit after that, each stuck in our own thoughts. Ettie's apparently is about leaving, because it's not long before she once again pleads for me to let her go.

"You have to let me out here, Leo. It's the only way you or your friend will be safe."

"I'm not letting you go, Ettie."

Before I saw her again, I couldn't truly tell you what my end-game was here. I didn't want her mother hurting her, but I didn't think beyond that. Now, after seeing her, factoring how my body comes alive near her—a feat that has never happened before—I can admit my reasons for holding onto her are much more selfish. Being close to Ettie makes me feel...*alive*.

"Then, you'll die—or worse."

"There's worse than death?" I ask, smiling at the forlorn tone to her voice.

"If you have to ask that, you must have forgotten what my mother can do to someone," she says quietly, staring out the window.

Rage fires up inside of me without warning, my grip tightening on the steering wheel.

"I've forgotten nothing," I respond, my voice clipped with anger because I'm pissed off she would remind me of my past. The nightmares I have every night are enough. I don't need to be reminded of it while I'm awake.

Not by Ettie...especially not her.

15

Ettie

Over the years, I've dreamed of seeing Leo again. None of those dreams were like this, however. We haven't talked in at least ten minutes. I don't try to start a conversation, because I heard the anger in his voice earlier. Years might have passed, but it's clear my mother has left her mark on him. He has no idea that she left the same marks on me, maybe worse ones—at least physically, because I don't think Leo scars. At least, I've never seen any on him. Now that I'm older, I look at my dreams differently. I know now that people don't normally drink blood, like Leo did when he was at the lab. I guess that makes him what people call a vampire. He's definitely not like the ones in the movies though. Leo wasn't born and then died only to have been bitten and come back. I know that much. He had never lived outside of the lab until the day he escaped. Which is why me being with him is a really bad idea. The last thing Leo needs is to be caught again. You would think that he'd know that, but I'm not going to argue with him. To be honest, he kind of intimidates me. I would have to be a fool not to see the anger that he has festering inside of him. Getting free from my mother did nothing to put the past to rest for him. I don't guess it would, but I had hoped he found peace. That's the one thing he wanted most in his dreams…

We pull into the parking lot of a small motel. There's a neon sign above the vehicle and shining down with a pale pink glow, because the sign is faded and not bright at all.

Cornerstone Motel.

Underneath that, about five feet down the pole, there's a handmade, wooden sign.

Cheap Rooms.

I know this place, actually. I came here looking for a room. Their idea of cheap and mine are very different, so I've been crashing at the shelter. I have to always make sure I have enough for a quick bus ticket out of town. Once I buy a bus ticket tonight, I won't have anything left over. I hope where ever I end up, I manage to find a job pretty quickly. That's after I manage to get away from Leo. The prospect exhausts me just thinking about it.

Leo pulls into the parking lot and turns his car off. I look around, expecting to see one of his friends, but no one else is around.

"Where is he?" I ask, frowning and wondering if some of my mother's goons found him.

"Who?"

"Your friend? You said we were meeting him, right?"

"Yeah, but he'll be in the room. Let's go."

"The room? Uh…I'll just wait here," I respond, slightly nervous. It's not that I think Leo would hurt me, I don't. I'm not ready to go into a hotel room with him either. Plus, I need to get away from here. I'm sure my mother has more people in the area. For all I know, she's here herself. I need to keep moving.

"That's not an option, Ettie. If I leave you out here, you will run. Then I'll spend another month hunting you down again. Now, make this easy on me and get out on your own, instead of forcing me to carry you inside."

"Carry me?" I ask, my body flushing warm at the thought.

"Exactly and no offense, you weigh more than you did five years ago."

"I…" I stop, because whatever I was going to say dies on my tongue. *I weigh more?* "Did you just call me fat?" I gasp, wondering if he would kill me if I kicked him in the balls.

"I didn't say that. But you can't argue you definitely weigh more than you did when we last saw each other," he says, and he's got this cocky smile on his face that might be cute, but I really want to slap it off of him.

"I was a kid," I snap and for some reason that makes him laugh.

"I'm just playing with you, Ettie. Superhuman strength here, remember? I can lift you and twenty others just like you, easily."

"Twenty? Now you might be stretching it," I mumble, blushing for some reason.

"Let's get out, Sunshine. I'll introduce you to Seven."

"Seven? It's been over five years. Shouldn't everyone have normal names by now?"

"We haven't quite figured out what normal is yet, Ettie. C'mon. It's time to stop stalling."

"I'm not stalling," I lie. "I just think it would be better if you let me go now. My mother undoubtedly has more men either already here, or on their way. It would be safer for all of us if I leave town tonight."

"You will, as soon as we take care of a few things."

"I meant alone," I mutter.

He lets out an irritated breath of air. If he thinks I've aggravated him already, he probably hasn't seen anything yet. I don't bother telling him that, however. I doubt it would do any good. Just like I'm positive that if I don't walk to the hotel room he will carry me. That's what spurs me to undo my seatbelt and open the door. My legs are so wobbly when I stand, that my knees nearly buckle. I didn't realize exactly how much everything that just happened affected me. I brace myself on the side of the car, take a couple of deep breaths and then take off walking. I have no idea where I'm going. The hotel rooms are all outside, with the office the first room and every room after that one is one you stay in, making an 'L' shape layout.

Leo reaches over, grabs my hand and takes it in his. Instant heat swarms me and my knees go weak yet again. I even stumble and Leo's hold increases, his other hand coming to my side. He steps into me, so close that I can smell his aftershave and the scent is intoxicating. I'm not sure I've ever smelled anything better in my life.

"Are you okay?" he asks, his voice husky and soft. His head is bent down as he looks at me and I drop our connection, afraid that if I keep looking into his eyes, he will see the way I'm reacting to him. I don't really want that, although I'm positive he already knows.

"Yeah," I murmur, licking my lips nervously, my head down. I take a breath to try and steady my nerves and finally look up. "It's been a rough last hour."

He nods and it looks like he might buy that as the reason I'm acting so strange. I hope he does, because I honestly have no idea how to explain why Leo seems to make my hormones rage like I am just hitting puberty all over again.

When we make it to the door, Leo knocks on it in a quick refrain that is almost like a drum beat. I'm sure it's some kind of signal. In just a minute, the door opens and the guy inside stands back letting us in.

"I was beginning to wonder if you were going to make it. Thought the assholes might have captured you," the guy growls, the anger in his voice sounding a lot like Leo's. *If they're so upset they have to be here, then why did they come?* I only think the question, I'm not stupid enough to say it out loud. When we get inside, Leo closes the door and the sound seems abnormally loud. I do my best not to jump. I turn around and face the two men, ignoring the panic that is trying to take root deep inside of me. Leo won't hurt me. *He won't.* I'm not so sure about the man standing across from him, however. Everything about the other guy screams anger. He's tall, at least a couple of inches taller than Leo—and Leo towers over my five-seven frame. He's just as broad too, but somehow, he's even more deadlier looking—if that's a thing. He's harder, his voice grittier and he makes me nervous just being around him.

"Hell, no. I wouldn't let that happen. I'd set myself on fire first," Leo says, and I don't think he's joking. My eyes go round at the thought and a chill runs down my spine.

"Let me grab our shit and we'll head—"

"Before we do that, we have a slight problem," Leo says, stopping the man from moving or finishing his sentence.

"What's that?" I ask, right along with the other guy—for the life of me, I can't remember what number Leo called him. Leo looks at me and for some reason smiles, before shifting his gaze back to his buddy. I don't know what there is to smile about. I sure as hell don't feel like smiling.

"She has some kind of chip implanted and she thinks that is how they keep finding her."

"Keep finding me? You know—"

"I've been trying to find you since almost the day you ran away from your mom's, Ettie," he says, surprising me. I don't know what to say, so I remain silent.

"If her mother put it in there, it probably is. It's probably also hardwired to explode, just like Nine's was."

"Explode?" I cry out in shock.

"Damn it, Seven, quit blurting shit out," Leo growls, his hand coming over to capture mine and pull my body into his. I don't fight it, I'm too busy panicking and dealing with the fact that there's something inside of me that could potentially explode. I don't know why that didn't occur to me sooner. It sounds just like something my mother would do. My body begins trembling and I can't stop it. Leo wraps his arms around me, kissing the top of my head and leaning down to whisper into my ear. "It's going to be okay, Ettie. I'm not going to let anything happen to you. I promise." I don't know why his simple words make me feel better, but they do. I put my hands on each side of his shirt and hold onto him like that. It seems safer than putting my arms around him.

"Yeah, but don't worry, if you haven't exploded yet, chances are it's a dud. All of ours were, except for Nine's." He's quiet for a minute and I see pain on his face. I don't ask questions, but I want to.

"Either way, it has to come out," Leo says. "Get the alcohol and I'll get things ready in here."

"Sounds good."

"Get things ready?" I squeak, not liking the sound of this—of *any* of this.

"We're going to take it out. Don't worry, Ettie. We were prepared for this because of what happened to us."

"I...*You're* going to take it out?"

"Yeah."

"Did you happen to go to medical school in the last five years, Leo?"

"Medical school?"

"You know, that thing where they train you to go in and do surgery? Because if not, there's no way you're getting near me."

"I haven't gone to medical school, Sunshine," he laughs, which is annoying. He's cute when he laughs, but there's definitely nothing to laugh about right now.

"Then you aren't cutting my head open," I state, my tone brokering no argument. I cross my hands at my chest, daring him to try it.

"Just the back of your neck," Leo's friend interrupts. "And luckily for you, it won't be very deep."

"It doesn't matter, because you aren't taking it out," I tell him, shaking my head.

"So you'd rather just have a ticking time bomb in your head?" Seven replies and I wince.

"Damn it, Seven—," Leo growls, but I just keep pushing through, making note of the jerk-face's name, or number really.

"Yep. I would," I tell him, lying, but not about to step down. I don't trust him to operate on me. I mostly trust Leo, despite not answering me when I needed him most, but I don't want him cutting into me either.

"Okay then, have it your way. The bitch is riding in your car, Leo. I'm not about to get brain matter in my Vette."

I can't stop the audible gasp that comes out at the picture Seven paints, but it's more than that.

Leo turns so quickly that his body is a blur. One minute I'm in his arms and the next he's all the way across the room, his hand around Seven's neck, pinning him against the wall. The sheetrock is cracked in the outline of Seven's body, too—proving Leo wasn't lying about his strength and also that he's extremely pissed.

"You will never call her a bitch again. Her name is Ettie," Leo says, his voice sounding inhuman.

"Get your hands off of me, Brother," Seven orders, his voice deadly, though not as animalistic as Leo's.

I can't see Leo, his back is to me, but I can see Seven's face and the anger blazing from him is almost as frightening as the way his eyes turn bright yellow. *Yikes.*

"Actually, my name is Esther," I call out, my voice high pitched. "I've always hated it. I thought about changing it, but I mean I've had the name my whole life. What else would I be called? I'd be silly with a name like Beyoncé, plus I can't even sing. That means Celine is out, too. I could probably use Martha, but that's almost as bad as Esther," I ramble, trying to defuse the moment before war breaks out. It seems to work because both men turn to look at me and Leo seems at least a little more relaxed. Slowly, his hand drops from Seven's neck and I figure that's good.

"Martha, Sunshine?" Leo asks and it dawns on me that he seems to have given me a nickname. It's kind of pretty and it makes me feel happy. Perhaps the chip in my head is already doing damage, because I must be insane.

"Yeah, like Martha Stewart? I mean, I'm sure she's nice and things, but she seems boring. Although she has been to jail, so what do I know? It was one of those plush jails I'm sure, but still she was there. That means she served hard time. So, maybe she's not boring."

"Sunshine?"

"Yeah?" I ask, glad to stop talking because I ramble when I get nervous and I'm definitely rambling right now.

"Shut up," he says and I scrunch my nose up at him, not liking that he told me to shut up, but doing it all the same because I really want to stop talking.

"Who's doing the cutting?" Seven asks and I wince, and I want to argue some more, but I'm afraid if I do they'll go back to wanting to kill each other. I mean, they said that they've done this before, right? Didn't they? Shit, I can't remember. But, obviously they had their own taken out and they're still here. That has to be a good sign…*Right?*

Yep. I'm definitely panicking. I take off running toward the door. Leo wraps his arms around me and captures me before I get there.

Shit.

16

Leo

"Woah, Sunshine," I purr into her ear, holding her body tight against me—her back to my chest. My arms are locked around her and this scent wraps around me. It reminds me of warm sun on a Summer's day. It's the first thing I remember after I got my freedom and every single time I get near Ettie it's the same fragrance.

"I don't want to do this, Leo," she says, her voice laced with so much panic that it sounds as if she's in pain. It tears at my heart. I would have thought I didn't have one, but I've always had a soft spot for Ettie. *Always*.

"I know, Sunshine, but we have to get it out. It might hurt a little, but I'll be very careful," I promise her, vowing to do just that.

"You're going to do it?" Her voice squeaks, as if she can't believe what I just said. Her breathing is shallow, causing her to pant as if she's run a hundred miles.

"I won't allow anyone else to touch you if I can help it, Ettie. I know you're worried, but remember, I was created to be a soldier. That means I have detailed information about the human anatomy."

"You do?" she asks, sounding hopeful for the very first time.

"I do, and I have a medical kit with me. We all keep one with us in our gear. It's going to be okay, I promise."

I slowly relax my hold and Ettie moves away from me. My body instantly misses her. My cock is hard, it didn't occur to me to try and hide it from her as her ass was pushed up against me. Did she feel me? Did it excite her? *Fuck.* These are not thoughts I should be having—at least, not right now. I need to concentrate on getting that damn thing out of Ettie and getting her as far away from here as possible.

"Leo?" she asks softly, turning around to face me.

"Yeah, Sunshine?"

"Do you have an x-ray machine in your medical bag? Because you don't even know where this chip is and there's no way I'm letting you just root around in my head until you find it," she insists, stubbornly, her brown eyes sparkling with anger and determination.

"Alright then," Seven says, coming up behind Ettie, putting his hand on the side of her face to angle her neck and then injecting her with a needle.

I snarl even as I see it, reaching out, ready to break his arm, but I can do nothing more than grab Ettie as her legs give out.

"Wha...what did he do?" she slurs.

"It's okay, Ettie. It's going to be okay," I promise her, looking into her eyes and hoping she can see enough there to trust me.

"He... drugged..." She doesn't get the words out before she's completely out. I pick her up and carry her to the bed.

"I told you not to fucking touch her," I growl.

"You were taking too long. We need to get out of here. I can feel them getting closer," Seven responds, his voice showing no emotion. I frown, looking up at him. We all have this sixth sense that warns us of approaching trouble. We've relied on it heavily, especially when fleeing the compound. I've been so wrapped up in Ettie and everything going on, I've ignored that, but it's clear that Seven hasn't.

"How long do you think?" I ask, as I turn Ettie over to give me a better view of the back of her neck.

"A couple hours? Maybe more, maybe less. It's not like we can put a clock to this shit, Leo," he mutters, annoyed.

"Turn your head," I order.

"You've got to be kidding me."

"Turn your damn head while I take her shirt off."

"What has gotten into you?" Seven asks, but he turns around just the same.

I frown. I take Ettie's shirt off as carefully as I can. I let my hand move along her back, her skin pale and unbelievably soft and warm…God, she's so warm it seems to heat my own body just from touching her. There are scars on her back, too. I move my finger carefully over one of them. It's whiter than the rest of her skin, letting me know that they've been there for a long time. They are small slivery lines that cross and intersect…I need to ask her about these when she's awake. I have a horrible feeling that I know what they are. If I'm right, I won't rest until Ettie's mother is dead.

"I don't know," I whisper quietly, unable to process how I feel or what's going on in my head.

I quickly pull the blanket up to the base of her shoulders, thankful her bra hides any side view of her breasts. I instinctively know I couldn't handle it if Seven could see that.

I'd have to kill him.

"Whatever it is, you need to get a handle on it. Jesus. I thought you were going to go through an anatomy lesson with her, just to make her feel better."

"I didn't lie to her. We do know the human anatomy, probably better than a doctor," I mumble.

"Were you going to explain that you know the anatomy of a human so you know the best ways to kill someone?"

"Fuck off," I mutter, unzipping the small container that holds tweezers and a scalpel. That's another thing that I didn't lie to Ettie about. All of us have medical kits. We might be hard to kill, but a well-placed bullet can cause us to bleed out quickly. We all have rudimentary skills, to do primitive surgery. I never minded it before, but looking down at Ettie, I hate that I'm not more adept in my knowledge now.

Seven is still laughing at me, the asshole. I look down at Ettie's body, hating what I have to do next, but knowing it can't be helped.

"Ow..." I open my eyes slowly, a wave of nausea hitting me so strong I moan.

"How are you doing, Sunshine?"

I wince because Leo's voice sounds so loud. I force my eyes open to look up at him.

"Sick to my stomach," I mumble.

"I'm sorry." His hand brushes the side of my face and it feels nice, but I ignore it. I can't believe his friend drugged me and Leo let him.

"Where are we?" I ask, realizing we're in a car and driving down the road.

"Somewhere in Arkansas, about to pull over for supplies and gas. Are you hungry?"

My stomach lurches at the mere mention of food and I move my hand to hold it—as if that will help settle it.

"Ew, no food," I mutter weakly.

"Maybe some ginger-ale?" he suggests. I hate ginger-ale, but I've heard that does help, so I shrug and then whimper when it causes pain. I hiss deeply, my hand going to the back of my neck where there's a bandage. Anger wells up inside of me. I know it needed to come out, but even as I feel relief, I'm mad because they did it without my permission. Heck, they did it knowing I expressly told them not to.

"I'm sorry, Baby, does it hurt?"

I ignore the warmth the endearment gives me and look out the window. I don't respond. There's no point.

In a few minutes we pull into a gas station. It's really early in the morning. I can tell because the sun is barely peeking out of the clouds. I already have my seatbelt undone by the time he stops the car. That means the moment he puts it into park, I'm outside, walking toward the door to the station.

"Woah, there. Where are you going?" Seven asks, coming out of nowhere.

I focus all of the anger I have on him, and there's a lot. I try to forget that he's been created with powers and skills meant to kill me. Right now he's just an asshole who is the cause of my pain.

"I need to go to the restroom, I'm sick to my stomach," I explain through clenched teeth.

"Awe, need to go off to puke, huh? Sometimes the medicine can do that if you're a lightweight," he says and the asshole doesn't even bother to hide the laughter in his voice.

"I wouldn't have this problem if you hadn't injected me with junk and operated on me without my permission," I respond, bitingly, narrowing my eyes at him because he's really a jerk and I wish I had the courage to hit him. It might not hurt him, but it would make me feel better.

"Ettie," Leo says, coming up from behind us. Immediately his hand goes around my back to rest on my side. I don't think it's about holding me back from his friend, it feels like affection. I shouldn't like that, but I do—even sick. I remind myself however, that he's probably doing it because he still sees me as the little kid I was when he was imprisoned. I ignore how sad that makes me feel.

"It's against the law to do that to me you know," I mumble, still giving Seven the stink-eye. "I should have you both arrested," I tell them, my stomach lurching again. I *really* need to get to the restroom, I pull against Leo's body, but he doesn't let me go.

Seven outright laughs at me. "Do you really think scaring us with the police and your silly laws will intimidate us, Esther?" He shakes his head, looking at me like I'm an idiot and kind of making me feel like one. "Leo, I think you might have scrambled her brains when you operated on her," he adds, still laughing. That's when I stop fighting. He wants to be an ass, then fine. I quit holding back the bile that wants to rise and I let it go, vomiting all over Seven's shoes. I might've felt guilty, but I can't...I'm too busy being sick.

"I can't believe she threw-up all over my loafers. Those damn things were made of Italian leather. They cost over six hundred bucks."

"Get them cleaned," I laugh, because Seven looks so damn sad as if he's in mourning over a damn pair of shoes.

"You can't clean Italian leather. They're ruined," he huffs. I look down at the cheap flip-flops he grabbed at the gas station and don't even bother to laugh.

"She warned you she was sick," I remind him, enjoying this probably far more than I should.

"Whatever. We're stopping at the first shoe store I find. There has to be a mall around here somewhere."

"We'll stop, only if it's on the way. I don't see how LaDawna or her henchmen can follow us now, but I'm not taking a risk. We need to get back home quickly."

"Agreed," Seven mumbles, clearly not happy, but at least we're on the same page.

"Hi…" Ettie says, looking a little better when she opens the door to the restroom and finds us standing there.

"Feeling better?" I ask her, concerned. She looks really pale and her eyes have some major shadows.

"Yeah. I'd kill for a toothbrush, though," she mumbles. "I rinsed my mouth out, but…yeah."

I produce the small travel pack I had Seven pick up at the store from behind my back. "Your wish is my command," I tell her, gently handing it over to her.

She takes it, staring down at it in shock.

"Thank you," she whispers.

"Anything for you, Sunshine. Now, go clean up and we'll see if you can handle any food.

"Uh…just some ginger-ale and maybe a pack of crackers?" she says, looking over her shoulder at me, when she turns to go inside.

"You got it," I tell her and wait for her to close the door.

"I uh…I'm sorry," she mumbles to Seven. He gets a stubborn look on his face as if he'd like to swat her like a fly. I elbow him—none too gently.

"It's fine. I needed a new pair of shoes anyway," he mutters. Ettie looks down at his feet and back up at him.

"You have pretty toes," she says, and there's signs of life in those brown eyes, but I'm too busy dealing with jealously over the fact she just told Seven his toes were pretty.

What in the fuck is wrong with me?

"Go finish cleaning up, Ettie," I grumble. She looks over at me confused, but closes the door. Seven starts laughing.

"What are you laughing about now?"

"You're jealous your little girlfriend thinks my feet are sexy."

"*Pretty*—and it was your toes. No one could think those ugly things you have are sexy."

"You really are jealous," he laughs. I want to deny it, but honestly can't.

"I know," I mutter, scratching my jaw. "I don't know what in the fuck is wrong with me. Our kind don't get jealous. Hell, we don't even get attracted to others. You know that as well as I do."

"You're attracted to her."

"Fuck, yeah. She even makes me hard."

"Hard?"

"Like a fucking rock," I mutter, feeling uncomfortable.

"You mean…" Seven looks at me in shock—the same shock I've been feeling since seeing Ettie again. This isn't anything new to us. Since we gained our freedom, we've studied human behavior and we knew anatomy already. Men are attracted to women, sometimes other men and sometimes both. It's elemental and animalistic—which is what we were created after…animals. By all accounts, we should have extremely high sex drives and yet…not a one of us has ever felt the need to mate, to find a partner. We assumed it was a gene that LaDawna and Draven learned to isolate and take out of our DNA, because it could be deemed a weakness. We accepted that suspicion as fact. Why wouldn't we? We couldn't even be upset about it. How can you miss something you never had, or even experienced? But, boy have I experienced it seeing Ettie again. I'm trying to get my head clear so I can get her back to safety, but my aching cock and balls definitely have other ideas.

"I mean I want her. You know as well as I do what that means."

"Suddenly I'm jealous of you," Seven says and I shake my head.

"Don't be. Just because I want her, it doesn't mean it's mutual. She knows what kind of monsters we are. Do you really think she wants to tie herself to that, Seven?"

He doesn't answer.

There's really nothing for him to say.

19

Ettie

"You're attracted to her."

"Fuck, yeah. She even makes me hard."

My body feels like it's on fire. I wasn't meant to overhear what Seven and Leo were talking about, I know that.

But I did.

And now I don't know how to unhear it. My mind is whirling and my heart is beating erratically. I used to dream about the day that I would get older and Leo would fall in love with me. I let go of that dream years ago, when he told me he couldn't help me…when I lost the ability to enter into people's thoughts or dreams…when I couldn't talk to Leo anymore. Is that back, now that Leo has removed the chip? The urge to try it is there, but I'm afraid. I'm not ready to find out. I think the disappointment might…kill me.

"You've been awfully quiet since we left the gas station," Leo says, pulling me out of my thoughts. I shift uncomfortably in my seat, because I've been quiet since I heard what he said about me. I can't explain that, however.

"I don't have much to say," I murmur, hoping I pull off sounding bored. "When are we stopping for the night?"

"We're probably not. You can sleep while I drive."

"You can't drive through the night. It's too dangerous," I argue.

"Not for me, I can go three or four nights without sleep, as long as I'm not injured, Sunshine."

"Oh. That's kind of sad."

"It is?" he asks, sounding shocked.

"Yeah. I think one of my favorite things to do is curl up under clean sheets after a stressful day. I've missed it."

"Missed it?"

"I've been staying at shelters. Usually a cot for my bed and a blanket, but I mean, I always keep my clothes on and well, it's not the same as when I was at home…"

"Did you sleep without your clothes at home?" he asks and I know I'm blushing, I don't even have to look to know my face is beet red.

"Weren't there others in the house?" he asks, his voice has a harsh tone in it that I can't remember hearing from him before. I shiver in response, unsure of what to make from it.

"Amelia, my nanny. If Mom wasn't home, sometimes Clive would stay inside as a guard."

"Clive?" Leo asks, his voice deadly. "You were naked in your bed with a man in the house?"

"I kept my door locked." In response, Leo let's out a sound that reminds me of a bear growling. "I was perfectly fine," I mutter.

"You were not. You were stupid. It's a wonder he didn't break in and rape you."

"Will you stop!"

"I will not. From here on out, you will not sleep naked unless I'm in bed beside you." He barks out the order, sparing me a brief glance before turning his attention back to the road.

"Uh, Leo…you aren't sleeping in bed with me." He doesn't respond, he just looks at me and I feel panic explode inside of me. "I mean it! We can't share a bed."

"Why not?"

"Why not?" I repeat, wondering if I can pinpoint the exact moment that my life seemed to go off the rails.

"Exactly, why can't we share a bed?"

"Because…we're not married."

"You don't have to be married to share a bed, Ettie," he laughs, his attention going back to the road.

"Okay, maybe not, but you should at least be in a relationship," I respond, trying to reason with him.

I should have known better.

"I'd say you and I have a relationship. We've known each other since you were a child. You're definitely not a child now, Ettie."

I swallow, at the glint in his eye when he glances over at me. I get these heated tingles running through my body, zapping me like little electrical currents.

"I meant a sexual relationship," I mumble, refusing to look at him when I say the word sexual.

"It will happen."

It's just three words, but those words take my breath.

"It can't," I repeat, stubbornly.

"It can and it definitely will. Don't pretend you didn't hear me tell Seven that I wanted you, Ettie. The minute you came out of the bathroom I could tell you heard me. There's no point in pretending about it now."

"I have no idea what you're talking about," I mumble, turning my attention to the scenery outside my window, but in reality, the landscape just blurs.

"Liar."

"I don't want to play games with you, Leo."

"That's good, because neither do I, Ettie. I'm in new territory here. I've never wanted anyone before the way that I want you. That's not a line or a game, it's a simple truth. I think you're attracted to me, and I think there's enough between us to see where this attraction goes and that's what we're going to do."

"I don't remember agreeing to any of this."

"You will."

"I'm just as positive that I won't. You don't even know me, Leo."

"I do. Don't tell me you forgot the friendship we shared, Ettie. I owe you my freedom. Hell, I owe you my life."

"I don't want a relationship with you because you feel some sense of duty."

"Good, because that's not what we're doing."

"We're not doing anything. Until last night, I hadn't even heard from you in over five years. You can't just waltz back into my life and expect me to start a relationship with you."

"Why?"

"What do you mean?"

"Why can't we start a relationship? We're attracted to each other. There's no one else in our lives. Why can't it work, Ettie?"

"I don't want to talk about this," I mumble.

"It's a simple question, Sunshine."

"How about the fact that I don't trust you anymore?"

"You don't…Why in the hell not? I'm here saving you from your mother. I came to save you, Ettie."

"I didn't ask you to. I didn't even want that. I'm an adult now, Leo. I can save myself."

"You said yourself that one day your mother would find you. Ettie, you needed me, whether you're willing to admit it or not."

"She may have, but if she did, I would have handled that on my terms, too. If you don't depend on anyone, you don't have to be disappointed when they let you down."

I didn't mean to tell him that, it's definitely saying too much. I can't stop myself though. If he's going to say outlandish things like he wants a relationship with me, then I need to protect myself. I need to remind my heart that I'm alone in this world.

I always have been. Leo talks a good game, but when the chips are down…

"Who let you down, Baby?" Leo asks so softly, his voice so tender that my heart feels like it twists inside of my chest.

I ignore him, not responding, and after a few minutes I hear him let out a frustrated breath. He doesn't press the subject though, and I'm glad. I lean my head against the glass of the passenger window and close my eyes. I hear his soft voice again, so gentle and caring.

"Who let you down, Baby?" I hear again in my head.

I feel myself drifting off to sleep and although my guard is down, I don't reply...at least not out loud.

"You did, Leo."

Y*ou did, Leo.*
We've been on the road for two days. If I could take a direct route back, we'd already be there. We're zig-zagging and taking as many backroads as we can, however. I don't know how far of a reach Draven has. We can't put our new compound at risk though. We're not ready. I also can't put Ettie in danger and that means even if it takes me longer, I'm being very careful to cover our trail. Tonight I broke down and stopped at a motel. Seven wasn't happy, but then again, he's never happy.

The last twenty-four hours, I've been reserved with Ettie and I know she's noticed the difference. She keeps staring at me and I can see the hurt in her eyes. I've not heard her voice in my head since she delivered those three words.

Those three bittersweet words.

They torture me, but hearing them brought such joy... because Ettie was talking in my head again. I never realized how much I had missed our connection. Just hearing her voice in my head again filled me with joy. Always before when she spoke, there was no joy to be found, but there was still comfort—even if she was a little girl. Now, it's euphoria, except for the sadness and pain in her words.

"I thought you said we weren't stopping."

I yank my gaze back to Ettie, shaking off my thoughts and instead concentrating on her.

"You didn't rest well in the car. We have more distance between us and Tennessee now. I think it's safe to let you crash in a real bed for one night."

"Where are we anyway? You are taking so many backroads I'm losing track. I swear I think we passed into the state line of Oklahoma three times today," she mumbles, obviously tired.

"That's because we did. I don't want to leave a clear trail that Draven might follow. I don't know how far his reach is, but these days you can tap into video cams easily. We're in Arizona, tomorrow we'll drive north. If you are doing okay, we'll drive straight into Montana."

"Is that where we're going?" she asks and I realize I've never told her. I've not discussed much at all with her. Yet, she's still going. Surely that means she trusts me, even if it's just a little.

"Yeah, Sunshine. You'll be safe there. Our bunker is in the side of a mountain and no one knows it even exists. The men we hire to work are kept isolated and when it's time, we'll wipe their memory."

"Wipe their memory?" she asks, alarmed and I sigh. I probably shouldn't have told her that. I forget sometimes around Ettie. I'm comfortable with her and therefore, my guard is down.

"It's not as bad as it seems. Each of us seems to have a certain skill set. Some are the same and some are different," I tell her, sitting down on the bed beside her.

She had taken a shower earlier, that was an exercise in torture. Knowing Ettie was naked in the shower, water moving over her body nearly drove me insane. I held it together, but it sure as hell wasn't easy. Now she's in the bed, wearing my shirt...I'm not sure why the fact she's in my shirt should make me feel like I've won a huge victory in an epic war, but it does. She's under the covers, the covers pulled up to her chest, and her dark curls fanned out against her pillow. She's fucking gorgeous and I want her more than I've ever wanted anything in my life—including my freedom. It's completely unreal to me, but I'd give up my precious freedom and gladly go back into captivity for one taste of Ettie.

"Leo?"

"I'm sorry, what did you say?" I ask her, turning my attention back to the here and now and not my fantasies.

"I asked what your skills were?"

I frown, thinking about it.

"My strength and speed, although all of us have that."

"Is that it?" she asks and I try not to be offended, but the thought that she could find me lacking is annoying as hell.

"I assure you that I am more than capable of defending you, Ettie."

"I didn't mean that, Leo. I was just curious about you, that's all," she mumbles.

I stretch out beside her on the bed, and although I'm fully dressed and on top of the covers, it feels amazing to be able to reach over, pull her so that her head rests on my chest and take her into my arms.

"I'm fairly young, one of the last created. It could be that I've not grown into everything I'm supposed to have yet. Or maybe I have? I can't be sure, Ettie. I do know that Ten has just discovered he can short circuit anything with electricity. So maybe I've just yet to discover what I can do."

"Short circuit?"

"Yeah, with his mind, he somehow surges electricity at something until it overloads. It may not seem like much, but he can disarm security systems pretty easily and that's never a bad thing when you live life on the run."

"I suppose," she murmurs. "We shouldn't be lying in bed together," she says, yawning, the sound and her sweetness making me smile.

"I won't tell anyone, if you don't," I joke.

"You promise to stay above the covers?" she murmurs and I close my eyes as pleasure zaps through me, because I can feel her lips move against my t-shirt, heating the skin underneath with just her breath. For a man who has never experienced pleasure in his life, these small glimpses of it through Ettie are like heaven.

"I promise," I tell her, not truly wanting to, but not wanting to do anything that will stop how I feel right now. "I've missed you, Ettie," I tell her, kissing the top of her head.

"I've missed you, too."

I smile as her warmth floods my mind and I relish the words as she drifts to sleep. I don't think she realizes she's talking to me without voicing the words out loud yet. I have a feeling if she knew, she'd try extra hard to put that wall up between us. I don't want that. So, I'll just relish these small moments for now and try to find a way to get her to trust me, because the only thing I know is that I want Ettie...*Forever.*

21

Ettie

I wake up...*alone.*

My eyes dart across the room, instantly looking for Leo and he's nowhere. Panic hits me immediately. Has my mother caught us? There's no way Leo would leave me alone...would he? Five years is a long time. I don't really know Leo anymore. Not to mention that when I was terrified and he had his freedom, he didn't come for me. He told me no when I needed him the most. Now he's back and supposedly he's attracted to me. I want to believe him...*Am I fooling myself?* Since he's not here, maybe I am. I get up from the bed slowly. My hand goes to the pillow beside me, but it's cold. Clearly, Leo has been gone for a while and apparently, I'm an idiot. I walk to the bathroom, and no one is there. I pull the curtain away from the tub and it's empty. I breathe a little easier. If my mother was here, she'd be in this room. I doubt she would be hiding—more like holding a gun on me—but, I still feel better after checking. I go back to the main door and it's locked, but the deadbolt isn't secure now. Of course you can only do that from the inside and obviously Leo left. I reach up and secure it and then make my way back to the bathroom.

I'll take a quick shower and then maybe look around town. If I'm lucky, I can find a waitressing gig somewhere for a few days and build up some of my funds. I can also check out the local homeless shelters. It doesn't matter if Leo is gone. I've been on my own for a while now. I can take care of myself.

After my small mental pep talk, I adjust the shower and then hop in. I wash quickly, partly because being here alone leaves me unnerved and partly because I want to leave, in case Leo gets a guilty conscious and decides to come back. I don't want him feeling pity for me. I don't need anyone feeling that. I'm fine.

I'm more than fine.

As I'm toweling off, a thought occurs to me as I pad the tender spot on my neck that has stitches. It has a bandage over it, but I can feel it peeling. I probably wasn't supposed to get it wet. Oh well. Hopefully the bandage kept it mostly dry. I make a mental note to try and find some cheap bandages while I'm out. I doubt Leo left his medical kit behind. He probably took it with him to perform more surgeries on unwilling patients. My hand moves over the scars on my back. I can't feel them, the skin is numb, but I know they're there. I bet Leo took one look at them and decided he didn't 'want' me after all.

"Asshole."

"What did I do wrong this time?"

I stop drying my legs and raise up quickly, looking around for Leo when I hear his voice. It's stupid, because I know he's not there. It's been a while, but I remember how it used to feel when we would communicate like this.

"Get out of my head."

"You were in mine first, Sunshine."

"Well, I'm getting out of it now," I mumble. *"I didn't do it intentionally."*

"So, it's kind of like unintentional groping? I feel so used."

"I can't hear you."

"Liar."

"La, la, la."

"Unlock the door."

"How do you know it's locked?"

"Because I used the key and I still can't get in."

"I thought you left."

"I'm not going anywhere without you."

"I've decided to stay here. I'm going to go find a job today."

"Let me in, Ettie."

"No. I want you to leave. In fact, I'm demanding it."

"Open the door."

"We must have a bad connection. I want you to leave."

"I'm giving you one minute to unlock this door, Ettie. If you don't, I'm coming in."

"If you break the door, the management will know and they'll remember you."

"So?"

"You're keeping a low profile remember? So leave. This is where we part ways, Leo."

Silence and I feel the connection sever. I probably pissed him off, but I don't really care. There's no door being broke through in the other room, either. So, that's a good sign. Of course, he could be waiting for me outside. There's a small window in the bathroom. It faces the hill and it's on the backside, away from the parking lot. I'll leave through there, just in case.

With my plan in place, I quickly throw on my jeans and bra. I've barely slipped my t-shirt on when a hand wraps around my stomach and pulls me backwards. I let out a startled yell, just as Leo growls in my ear.

"You need to understand something right now, Ettie."

My heart is beating erratically in my chest and I'm trying to fight through my panic, reassuring myself that Leo wouldn't hurt me—at least not physically.

"What…" I have to stop and catch my breath before I can ask the question. "What's that?"

"I'm not letting you go. You're mine."

Now, I *really* can't catch my breath. In fact, I'm not sure I'm breathing at all…

22

Leo

"Leo, you need to let me go," Ettie says softly. Her voice is hoarse, and I don't think I'm imagining that she's excited. I may be making a mistake, a big one. Still, I can't make myself stop.

"I think I need to kiss you."

Then, before I can talk myself out of it, I put my hand on her neck, angling her where I need her the most and then lower my mouth to hers.

Instinct takes over. I've seen people kissing and I've definitely seen it on television. I've not once had the urge to kiss another, however.

Not until Ettie came back in my life.

At first, she doesn't respond and I immediately worry I'm doing something wrong. Then, almost shyly, the tip of her tongue grazes mine. I release a moan of pleasure into her mouth, because just that small touch explodes inside of me, bringing me so much satisfaction that I could drown in it—*drown in her*.

The kiss turns almost violent after that, because I'm desperate to have her, to taste her, to own her. She's right there with me, shyness disappears and instead she is kissing me back just as hungrily.

Eventually, we're forced to break apart, only to drag air into our lungs, our breathing so ragged that our breathing is all you can hear in the room.

"What was that?" she asks, her lips plump and swollen, her voice hoarse with hunger.

I laugh, startled at her question and the confusion in her eyes.

"That was a kiss, I'm pretty sure. I don't have much experience, but I think I did it right. If it's wrong, I don't really care, I enjoyed it too much."

Her fingers slowly move up to touch her lips, her brown eyes wide, dilated and looking at me in a mixture of surprise, shock, and awe. It's almost comical how a simple look like that after a kiss can make a man feel like a king.

"I've never been kissed before."

Possessiveness that I never knew I was capable of wells up inside of me and I find myself smiling.

"Good."

"Good?" she asks.

"I don't want you to have anyone's kisses but mine. Now, I know you won't."

"I'm not so sure that's a good idea, Leo."

"Are you saying you want to kiss someone else?" I ask, my voice little more than a growl at the idea of her wanting someone else.

"Of course not."

"But you want to kiss me, right?"

"I think it's time we talk about something else," she huffs.

"Fine. We'll talk about something else," I say, with a nonchalant shrug.

"That was easy," she mutters, confused.

"How did you get those scars on your back?" I ask her and

her face freezes for a second and then a look of panic moves over her.

"I've only wanted to kiss you my whole life, from the first moment your thoughts danced in my head, and I didn't even know what kissing was," she blurts out.

I let all of that sink in and then I throw my head back and laugh and as I do, one thought occurs to me.

I never laughed in my life until Ettie.

"Here. Drink this," Seven says, handing Leo a bottle of…
"Is that tomato juice?" I ask, kind of knowing better, but hoping I'm wrong. I look around the small diner that Leo brought me to. No one is looking like they're about to pull out crosses and wooden stakes. Chances are they believe it's just tomato juice purchased at the local gas station. That's what the label says…

"Well now," Seven says, sitting across from us. I'm in the booth seat, Leo's body pressed against me, staring at Seven and trying to forget I kissed Leo. I'm also trying to resist the urge to do it again. "That's what the bottle says, but I wouldn't place a bet on it. I swung by the local hospital and bag-snagged while I was there. It's been a few days since either of us have fueled up and who knows what lies ahead of us before we get home."

"Seven," Leo growls and he looks at me almost guilty.

"What? You said she knows what we are, right?" Seven says looking at me.

"I can talk, and yes I know. It's okay, Leo, I promise," I tell him, feeling guilty that I worried for a minute about anything. I just don't want others coming after Leo. It honestly doesn't bother me that he has to have blood to survive. I mean we all do, just…not like Leo exactly. He's still frowning and I put my hand over his. "Stop worrying," I tell him, squeezing his hand on reflex. Slowly his face softens and he relaxes. He squeezes my hand back and before I realize what he has planned, he kisses me again, although this is little more than a peck…

It still feels good.

When Leo pulls away, I can't stop looking at him. When I finally do glance away, I see Seven and he's studying me, a serious look on his face. I blush, and look down at my food.

"Shit, Seven did you taste this? It's horrible."

I jerk my gaze up to watch Leo.

"What's wrong?"

"This tastes like piss," Leo mumbles under his breath.

"Have you ever drank pee?" I ask, alarmed.

Seven laughs so loudly, several people in the small diner turn to look at us.

"It was a figure of speech, Sunshine," Leo replies, shaking his head. He's smiling at me with so much pleasure that I don't even mind that he's laughing at me.

"Oh," I mutter lamely and push a forkful of eggs in my mouth to keep from making an even bigger fool of myself.

"It tastes fine to me, better than fine really. Maybe your taster is off."

"Maybe, but I can't drink this shit."

"Dude, you're going to have to drink some soon. It's been a week."

"Don't you have to have it every night?" I ask, suddenly alarmed that Leo isn't taking care of himself. He seems so invincible, I never thought to worry about what would happen if he got sick.

"No, Sunshine. Just once every couple of weeks is mandatory, but after a week we can tell a difference in our strength and crap, so we try to limit to once a week."

"But you can eat regular food, right? I mean you're not just faking it so I'll feel comfortable eating in front of you?"

"We love food," Seven answers. "We just don't necessarily get any nutrients from it. For that…," he trails off, lifting his almost empty bottle up in salute.

"Gotcha," I reply, looking at Leo. "Then, you need to drink it."

"Ettie…"

"For me," I urge him, knowing that if Leo got sick, I couldn't handle it.

Leo stares at me and then with a resigned look he downs half the bottle. He gets such a grimace on his face that I wince. I'm pretty sure that means it's not good. I imagine that's the look on my face when I had to take medicine I hated.

"Fuck," he growls and Seven puts his bottle down and looks at Leo.

"Are you okay there, Man?" Seven asks and the concern in his voice would make me panic, if I wasn't already. Leo takes off without a word, practically running towards the bathrooms.

"Damn…"

"Do you think he's catching a cold or something?" I ask.

"I can't say, I've never seen this happen. None of us have ever gotten sick before."

"Never?"

"Not even a sneeze," Seven replies.

"I'm going to check on him," I mutter, even more scared now. I don't wait for Seven to reply, I walk to the bathroom. I stand awkwardly at the men's door and then knock.

"Leo, are you okay?" I ask. Seven comes up behind me and pushes the door open.

I cover my eyes quickly, afraid that there will be men lined up at the urinal. I've never seen a man naked before, and I'd rather the first time not be a bunch of strange men using the bathroom. I think that might scar me for life.

"You can look, Little One," Seven says, and despite the concern he feels for Leo, I can hear his laughter, too.

I slowly take my hand down and look into the bathroom.

Leo is leaning against the wall, clearly after being sick in the toilet. His face looks white as a ghost.

"Are you okay?" I ask him again, nervously taking a few steps into the room.

His eyes are closed and his breathing is ragged at best. "I must have caught a touch of a cold or something, Sunshine. I'll be okay."

"Seven says you guys don't get sick," I tell him, not buying his explanation.

Leo gives Seven a look and he just shrugs.

"I'll be fine," he says again and I don't wait, or even question myself. I run into his arms and hug him tightly. His arms come around me and the instant they do, some of my panic recedes. "I need you to be healthy, Leo."

"I'm fine, Ettie," he whispers against the top of my head.

"I...I care about you," I whisper. He doesn't reply and I worry I said too much.

"Then, I'm definitely going to be okay, Sunshine," he says, his voice thick. I pull away to look up at him. His hand comes down so he can brush his thumb against my lips. We stare at one another while he does that and I have to wonder if he's remembering our kiss...because I am.

"I'll go pay our bill, I already threw the bottles away," Seven mumbles.

"We've got to figure out what's wrong," I tell Leo when we're alone.

"Nothing is wrong."

I look at him, letting him know that I'm not buying that.

"Fine, we'll find out what's wrong," he says giving me a weak smile.

"If you get sick on me, I'll never forgive you, Leo."

"That doesn't sound quite fair," he laughs. He walks over to the sink, cups some water and rinses his mouth out.

"We're friends," I mumble. "I don't have to be fair."

"We're more than friends, Ettie," Leo responds, drying his

hands and then taking mine in his and leading us from the room.

"I'm confused about everything else right now. Friends seem…safer."

"I'm not confused. You're mine, Ettie."

"Yours? You make me sound like an old jacket or your car, Leo," I mumble, trying to hide the way his declaration excites me.

"Yeah, except I don't want to fuck my car," he whispers against my ear, his breath as hot as his words are dirty. I shiver in response, wondering if I'm getting in over my head, but unable to stop it.

I want Leo.

"Try this. You have to like it. It's AB Negative, this shit is liquid gold."

I narrow my eyes up at Seven. He's not wrong—the rarer the blood, it does seem sweeter. Looking at the glass he's handing me now, though, it doesn't appeal to me at all. The color looks almost dull, the stench alone is enough to make me gag.

I put the glass down in disgust.

"It's no use," I tell him, not even bothering to try. I already know it won't work.

"Shit. You've got to be kidding me."

"I wish I was. I can feel my body getting weaker even now, but the smell of that...," I move my hand toward the bottle, "is disgusting."

"Fuck," Seven replies and I nod.

"You can say that again. Did you call the others? Does Four have any ideas?" Four is kind of my last hope for figuring this shit out. He's been around longer than any of us, and lived on the outside with the others before him as part of Draven's unofficial army. He had freedom and Draven's blessing, until they rebelled against him and Draven captured them and imprisoned all of us, trying to figure out a way to rid us of any weaknesses and abolish our free will.

"He wanted to know if you'd been going dental while we've been out and about."

"Dental?" I frown.

"He wanted to know if you'd sank your fangs into a live specimen," Seven mutters guiltily.

"Absolutely not. That was part of our creed when we set up. The idea doesn't appeal to me anyway, but I'd do nothing that might bring attention to us. You know that."

"I do, that's what I told him," Seven mutters.

"But?"

"He says he's only seen this happen once long ago. When Two married a human."

"Two? One of the Elders?" I ask shocked. We've all heard stories of the first ones Draven created. They were the first four. Three are dead, leaving only Four remaining. Of all of us, he received the worst torture. Draven had him taken into his private chambers and doled out his punishment for hours upon hours. Sometimes it would last a week and the broken blob they would dump back into the containment cell didn't even resemble a human. It would take him months to recuperate and as soon as he began to do that…Draven would take him again. We're not sure how Four remained sane…some think he hasn't…at least, most of the time. He talks to himself all of the time and sees people who aren't there. It's freaky as hell, but we trust him and when he's lucid, he's not only the strongest of us, but clearly the wisest. If he can't help me now…

"Four was tired, so toward the end, the conversation kind of drifted," Seven says and I nod, understanding.

"Did he tell you anything? Did he say what happened to Two?"

"Is Ettie sleeping?" Seven asks, looking at the closed door. We are staying in a nice hotel suite tonight. Two separate bedrooms and one large sitting room with a pull-out couch and a small kitchen, which is where Seven and I are.

"She's sleeping. Quit stalling. Is whatever I have…" I stop, because after years of not caring if I lived or died, now that Ettie is in my life, I don't want to die. I want to live and I want to live with Ettie. "Is this what killed Two?" I ask, because until this moment I just assumed Draven killed Two, but maybe that's not true.

"He didn't say. Honestly, what he did say didn't make a lot of sense and if you haven't bitten a living person, I don't think it matters."

"Well shit…he had to have at least said something that has you spooked. I can tell by the way you're looking at me."

"He said he'd never heard of it from stored blood, but that maybe you found your mate, if you found blood outside of the bags we get from the donor centers and hospitals."

"My mate? What in the fuck does that mean?"

"He says that Two found his mate and married her. That he was bound to her by her blood."

"None of that makes sense."

"I told you it didn't. Soon after he began talking to himself again, so I'm not sure you can trust anything he said."

"Damn it," I hiss, rubbing my forehead and trying to dull the tension headache beginning to form.

"Listen, you said yourself that you didn't bite anyone or go outside our rules. You have nothing to worry about. I'm sure whatever this is will pass. We'll just keep trying and…"

"But, I did do something different," I confess, interrupting and looking up at Seven as reality settles in on me.

"…by tomorrow…What did you do?"

"I licked Ettie's wound on the back of her neck, once I took the chip out."

Seven stares at me in shock. I take a deep breath as I realize the truth.

Ettie's always been special. We've always had a connection

and I've always been drawn to her. Since getting her back in my life, my interest in her has changed and my reactions to her, wanting to kiss her, to make love to her, wanting things I've never wanted before in my life…it's all explained by three simple words.

Ettie's my mate…

Now if I just knew exactly what that means for my future. I stare at the glass of untouched blood and close my eyes.

Shit.

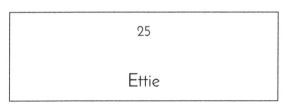

25

Ettie

*E**ttie's my mate.***
 Leo's words push firmly in my brain, waking me up as nothing else could. I may not have had a boyfriend or much of a social life for that matter, but I know what the word mate means. I've watched movies, and I read. I read a lot of romance about vampires and werewolves. It's my favorite past time really, especially after Leo disappeared. I'd be lying if I didn't admit that when I read those stories, I always imagined the hero in the book to be Leo and I was the woman he fell in love with. It was stupid and silly, but seemed harmless.

"Ettie's my mate."

I hear the words so plain that it wouldn't surprise me if Leo was standing beside me. The thing is, that although they do echo in my mind, Leo is saying them out loud now, telling Seven in the next room. Somehow, hearing him say it matter-of-factly, telling someone he trusts like that, makes it more real than anything else could.

My heart pounds against my chest as I get up and grab the hotel robe I took off earlier. I'm wearing Leo's shirt and it swallows me, falling almost to my knees, but I feel better covering up, knowing Seven is out there. I walk to the door as quietly as I

93

can. I open the door just a crack at first, half afraid that I've dreamed all of this. It'd be really embarrassing if none of it actually happened and I walk out there demanding to know what is going on.

"What in the fuck were you thinking?" Seven growls and I jump, thankful that I only cracked the door so that I can hide behind it.

"I wasn't thinking," Leo mumbles. "You don't understand…"

"You're damn right, I don't understand. We all took an oath, Leo!"

"I didn't bite her, damn it. I put the two stitches in, but there was a small drop of blood and…Fuck…"

"And you decided, gee it's there, I might as well drink it."

"It was one drop, not a glass damn it. I just licked her skin."

"And you signed your death warrant."

"Seven, don't be stupid. I just have to make myself drink the bags again. It will be okay."

"That sounds great, but did you forget what happened last time you tried to force yourself to drink? Because I sure as hell didn't."

"Just because it happened once, it doesn't mean it will happen again," Leo replies, but I can hear the worry in his voice along with the anger.

"You better hope it doesn't, because if not, you're a dead man, Leo."

"Seven—"

"What do you think is going to happen when Ettie finds out that you drank—"

"Licked, damn it!" Leo growls.

"*Licked* a drop of her blood and now you have to live off of her for the rest of your life and if she refuses, you'll die? How do you think she'll react to that, Leo? Because I got to tell you, I don't think she'll like it one damn bit."

"Damn it, Seven."

"I know you think you have a special connection with this girl," Seven sighs.

"I do," Leo insists.

"But, she's still a human and there's no way she's going to calmly accept that she's going to be chained to you forever because you did something stupid."

"I'm not going to tell her," Leo says and my heart feels like it freezes mid-beat.

"You're what?" Seven asks, as I'm struggling to breathe.

"I'm not going to tell her and neither are you."

"You're just going to pretend you're not dying? Or are you going to sneak in her room every night and drink from her like some damn parasite?"

"This is my problem. If I can't find a solution to it, I'll leave and Ettie will never know. I don't want her feeling responsible for me, or guilty because I'm dying."

"You're stupid if you think—"

"Whatever happens to me is not your business, Seven, anymore than it would be Ettie's fault if I die. I did this to myself and the hell of it is…"

"Is what?" Seven asks, stopping me from asking the question myself.

"I'd do it again. If all I ever have in this life is one kiss from Ettie and one taste of her blood, then that is better than anything I could ever have dreamed and it is more than enough."

"You're insane," Seven growls.

Leo shrugs in response and like a coward, I move back to my bed. There are things I need to talk to Leo about, but right now my mind is a mess. I need to have time to process all of this. So I go back to bed and I stay there, pretending to be asleep, even though I feel like I'll never sleep again. Later, when Leo climbs onto the bed and stretches out on top of the covers, I still pretend to be asleep. When he pulls me into his arms, I burrow against his chest and listen to his heart beat.

"Goodnight, Leo."

"Goodnight, Sunshine."

His voice echoes in my mind and there's so much simple pleasure in it that it's almost painful. Does he care about me? Or does it have something to do with the taste of my blood he took? I don't want Leo to be with me because he has no choice. How will I ever find out the truth and more importantly, will I be able to find out the truth before Leo runs out of time?

"Where's Leo?"

Seven is stretched out, his legs on a coffee table, his massive body on the couch, remote in his hand and he looks so bored that any moment his eyes might glaze over.

"He... uh..." Seven pulls his gaze up from the television to look at me. "He went out for a run," he mutters.

"I thought you guys said that you wanted to get an early start today?"

"He should be back anytime," Seven says with a shrug. "What are you so anxious for anyway? I thought you said that you were nervous about making it to the compound?"

"Well, I am. I mean my mother is directly responsible for the torture you guys lived with. I doubt everyone will be happy to see me."

"You were just a little girl. It's not like it is your fault, Ettie."

"Maybe, but other than Leo, I didn't even try to get to know the rest of you," I murmur guiltily.

"How would you have done that?" Seven asks and I frown.

"What do you mean?"

"Me, for instance. How would you have gotten to know me back then?"

"I don't know. I guess the same way I did with Leo."

"Which was?"

"I don't know he just…one day I heard him screaming in my head. I was doing my homework and I heard his pain…"

"Homework? I thought Leo said you were barely a baby when you first started talking to him?"

"I was five. My mother believed that homework is the key to being orderly and responsible."

"She's the reasons you have those scars on your back, isn't she?"

I take a step away from him in reaction. I narrow my eyes. "How do you know about those?"

His smile deepens. "I'm like Superman, Babe. I have x-ray vision. I can see you standing naked in front of me right now."

My arm goes up against my chest in defense, an audible gasp leaving my lips and Seven throws his head back and starts laughing.

"Oh shit," he cries. "If you could have seen your face." He shakes his head back and forth and continues laughing at my expense, I give him a look that's intended to dry his balls up like the Sahara Desert. For some reason, that just makes him laugh harder.

"Very funny," I mumble, so aggravated that the only saving grace is that I'm not blushing. I'm too annoyed with him. "I hope you're enjoying poking fun at me."

"You make it so easy," he says with a smirk.

"How do you know about them?"

"Leo mentioned it. I had to talk him out of going back and killing your mother. It wasn't easy."

"It wouldn't change the past," I tell him and he nods in understanding.

"Nothing can change the past," he says in agreement.

"Amen."

"So, how about you talk to me?"

"Uh, Seven, we are talking."

"I mean do that voodoo that you do with Leo. Talk in my head."

"I've never spoken with anyone before. I've explored other minds, but I'm not sure I want to do that with you."

"Why not?"

"You're annoying," I respond simply, thinking I could say more, but trying to be nice.

"You're scared," he says with a snort.

"Fine, I'll explore your head, but I swear if you're picturing me naked I'll short circuit your brainwaves and leave you drooling and peeing on yourself for the rest of your life."

"You can do that shit?"

"Not sure, but with you, I'd try it," I lie. As far as I know, I can't do it, but it's good to make Seven afraid, he's entirely too cocky.

"Okay, how do we do this?"

"Just let your guard down and I'll see if I can even find your brain and delve in."

"That hurts, Ettie," he mumbles, smirking at me.

"Shut up, I have to concentrate."

I close my eyes and reach out to Seven. I don't try to disguise it or hide what I'm doing. I have been able to do that in the past with my mom and a couple of others, but I don't want to hide it from Seven.

"Whoa," he says with a whistle, letting me know he can feel me pushing inside. He doesn't fight me and it's rather easy to slide in. It's also refreshing. There's no festering evil like in my mother's head. No hate, or resentment, like used to be so prevalent inside of Leo's mind in the beginning and there's no pain. He's straightforward. There's worry about Leo, and a sense of purpose to remain free and...

"You're lonely." I murmur into his head, waiting for his response. I register his surprise like it was my own. He thought he had that hidden and he wasn't expecting me to talk to him like this, even though he invited me to try. *"Try talking to me now.*

Just think it, don't speak." I instruct him and wait. I can feel his mind pushing, I feel his confusion and then finally frustration.

"It's not working," he says finally, with a large disappointed sigh. I sever our connection and sit down beside him.

"You could hear me," I remind him.

"Yeah, but you couldn't hear me and I really did try. So, maybe whatever this connection you have with Leo enables that."

"Could be," I answer. "He's out trying to find blood that doesn't gross him out, isn't he?"

"You've been eavesdropping, Ettie," Seven mumbles.

"I'm right, aren't I?"

"Yeah. He'll be back soon though."

"Because you don't think he'll find any."

"No, I don't."

"We'll give him a few more days, but if he doesn't have any success, you'll have to help me get my blood to him."

"It's not quite that easy, Ettie. I mean it's not like I've got a donor station or a lab set up. It's not so easy to tap your veins without it."

"You guys have that at the compound though, right? And we'll be there today. So, you have to help me."

"Ettie, Leo doesn't want that. He—"

"I won't let him die, Seven. Either you help me, or I'll find someone who will."

"You do care about him," Seven murmurs and I nod my head yes.

"I do."

"Then, when the time comes, I'll make sure to help."

"Good." We sit there in silence, Seven staring and then, frowning at me. "What?" I ask, getting irritated.

"If you tell anyone I'm lonely, I'll have to kill you," he mumbles. At one time, I might have been scared of him, but not now. Something's shifted between us, maybe because even before I explored his mind, his concern for Leo reached out to me.

"You can try it, but I've already sorted through and found the right brain synapsis to use against you. You'd never find your mate if you peed your pants all the time."

"You've been eavesdropping way too much, Little Ettie."

"You keep my secret, I'll keep yours."

I hold out my hand, waiting for his agreement. He stares at me and then rolls his eyes heavenward before reaching out and shaking mine.

"What the fuck is going on here?" Leo growls, as soon as the door opens. There's so much anger coming off of him that I can literally smell it.

Shit.

"Leo—" Seven begins, but Leo cuts him off.

"Let go of my Ettie's hand," he orders, his voice deadly.

My Ettie? Oh boy...

"Are you still upset with me?" Ettie asks.

"We'll be at the compound in about thirty minutes," I tell her, avoiding the question, and keeping my attention on the road, instead of her. Probably because my answer will make me sound like an asshole. Maybe I don't have any right to be upset, but I am. Hell, upset is too mild of a term for what I feel.

"You didn't answer my question," Ettie points out stubbornly.

"I don't like it," I finally say, my voice tight.

"Yeah, Leo, I gathered that. What I don't understand is why? It's not like I slept with him or even kissed him."

"It's a good thing, if you had I would have killed him."

"Oh, will you stop. Seven is your friend, your family kind of. You wouldn't have hurt him."

"And you're my woman. I would have absolutely," I tell her, not bothering to hide the anger anymore. Maybe it's good she knows. Maybe she'll begin to understand how serious I am about her.

Or go running for the hills because she's afraid of me.

"Leo, you're talking crazy. We shared one kiss..." Ettie's voice is filled with confusion and there's a hint of fear there as well. I want to tell her not to be afraid of me, but the truth is that when it comes to her, my emotions boil over. I honestly think that if she had kissed Seven, I would have killed him. I wouldn't have been able to stop myself.

"You forget the way I was created, Ettie," I mumble, not wanting to remind her, but at the same time, needing to make her understand.

"What do you mean?"

"I was made to be a soldier of war. Hell, they even spliced wolves into our DNA. That animal urge runs through me. If you think for one minute I wouldn't kill a man for putting a hand on you, you're wrong."

"Is this because you think I'm your mate?"

"Where did you hear that?" I growl. "Did Seven tell you that shit?"

"I heard you talking," she confesses.

"What else did you hear?" I ask, regret pooling in my stomach. I didn't mean for Ettie to hear me. I don't know how she'll respond to any of this and, if I am completely truthful with myself, I'm afraid to find out.

"Isn't that enough?" she asks, and I breathe easier. I don't want her to know that I tasted her blood. I don't want her to know that having it may be the key to my survival. That's not her burden to carry. If she chooses a life with me, that's different. She might be my mate, but she's human. There's no guarantee that I'm her mate. Hell, I don't even know if humans have mates. I've heard talk of soulmates, but general consensus I've found when researching it is that it is just bullshit and not real. In fact, since kissing Ettie, I've been researching a lot, and it seems humans tend to move from one relationship to the next, without looking back and going so far as to cheat on their mate with others, hurting them and destroying lives. I couldn't imagine ever doing that to Ettie. I'd kill myself before ever hurting her intentionally. It's hard for me to even reconcile the fact that Ettie is part of this race that I've been reading about.

It's almost enough to make me glad that I was created differently.

"Does it upset you that you might be my mate?" I hedge, wanting to know how she feels about it all.

"It upsets me that you might be drawn to kiss me because of some kind of chemical reaction in your brain and not because you actually like me," she mumbles, and when I glance over at her, she's looking out the window. I can see the profile of her face and the sadness there bothers me.

"Trust me, Ettie. I do *like* you."

"Maybe you do and maybe you don't, Leo. You don't really know me and now we'll never know if it is me you truly like, or just…"

"Fate?" I supply.

"Forced upon you. Maybe I'm only another prison, just a different kind," she says softly and her words make my heart hurt.

"If you're a prison, Ettie, then I'll gladly live in it, and if you think that choice isn't of my own free will, you're dead wrong."

"We'll see. Maybe your friend Four will know how to break the bond so that you can make a choice of your own free will, as you put it."

"I don't want it broken. I couldn't think of anyone I'd ever want in my life more than you, Ettie."

"Is that the compound?" she asks, changing the subject. I let her, but only because I have no idea how to make her understand.

My gaze goes up the mountain to the large stone structure at the top.

"That's it," I tell her, glad to be home and wishing I wasn't at the same time. I need more time alone with Ettie. I need to somehow make her understand.

I just wish I knew how to do that…

28

Leo

"How long will I have to stay here?"

I refuse to admit it's panic I feel when I hear Ettie's words. "What do you mean? Don't you like it here?" I ask, the thought never occurring to me that she might not.

"It's okay, Leo, but it's not how I see myself living. Most of this place is underground."

"How do you see yourself living?" I ask, sitting on the sofa beside her. My room is like a small apartment with a kitchen and living room open together, a hall that leads to a master bedroom with an attached bathroom. There's a small laundry room off the kitchen. To me—after living for so long in a small ten-by-ten cell, it felt like heaven. But, I don't know how Ettie lived before. It's starting to dawn on me that what I thought she would like, she might not.

"Well, I don't know, but I'm not one of you guys and this isn't practical for me. I'm going to need a job and I don't want to go back and forth from here all the time. It might inadvertently lead people to you. You might have gotten rid of the way my mother was tracking me, but I can't truly believe she will ever give up, Leo. It's not safe for me to be here."

My gaze moves to my front door. It's electric and slides back as another enters.

"She has a point."

I feel Ettie jump, and I pull her into my body on instinct. She doesn't fight that, at least, and I'm grateful. Ettie and I have so much to work through. I need to figure it out, right now, however, I'm forced to look at the man who came into my place without so much as a knock.

"Five, you knock when you come in, remember?"

"I figured you'd lock the door if you didn't want someone inside," he says, sitting in the chair across from Ettie and I. He centers his gaze on her and on instinct I let out a low, warning growl.

"You figured wrong. You need to leave. Ettie and I have some things to discuss."

"Go ahead, you won't bother me any," he says, his gaze not leaving Ettie.

"*Alone.*"

"But you've been alone, right? Shouldn't you have had time to discuss anything you needed to before getting here?"

"Stop," Ettie says, her voice cold as she sits up, pulling out of my arms. My gaze turns to her and I can see she's angry, but I'm not sure what's going on.

"Interesting, you do have a backbone, I was beginning to wonder."

"Quit trying to get inside my head."

"Amazing you can feel me there, most can't. Perhaps it's because you do it, too. Seven mentioned that's your special talent. Strange, don't you think?"

"Strange?" Ettie asks.

"That a mere human would have the same skill as I do."

"You're trying to get into Ettie's head," I growl, jumping off of the couch.

"You brought her here. She could put us all in danger again. I think I have a right to investigate," Five says, his voice calm.

"Maybe you should be more concerned why your major power is something so trivial a *mere* human has it, also," Ettie says, surprising me. I've always admired her courage, but right now she seems to have a fire in her that I hadn't truly noticed before. She's actually going toe to toe with Five and there's not a sign of fear in her. In fact, confidence is coming off of her in waves.

"Touché. You have a very strong will."

"Thank you."

"I'm not sure it was a compliment," Five responds.

"I think you should leave, Five."

"Eleven, surely you recognize that she brings danger with her. It wouldn't do for us to be discovered before we are ready to attack."

"As far as I know, we're not attacking. Did I miss something while I was gone? Four and the rest of us all voted to remain hiding from Draven and to live our lives in peace."

"If you truly think that's possible, you're more of an idiot than Four is. He's become weak and addled with his age. Draven needs to be destroyed," Five replies sternly.

I don't completely disagree with them, but at the same time, we're all tired and we need to regroup and actually get a chance to live. We've spent too long being imprisoned.

"His name is Leo, not Eleven."

"*Eleven* is not of your world, Esther. To think that you can mold him into it would be a grievous mistake."

"He may not be of this world, but if the goal is to blend in undetected from Draven and others like him, I would think adapting to this world would be key," Ettie replies and I smile.

"Perhaps," Five considers.

"If your number is five, aren't you near to the same age as Four?" Ettie asks.

"Yes," Five answers, a change moving over his face that I don't like. Before he was being antagonistic, but now there's an unreasonable anger coming from him that Ettie doesn't deserve and is kicking my senses into overdrive.

"Then, aren't you scared you'll become…how did you say it? *Addled* with your age?"

"The difference between Four and I, is that I've never been weak."

"I see," Ettie whispers.

"I think you might. I'll be keeping my eye on you, Miss Lane."

"Ditto, Scar."

"Scar?" Five asks, getting up to go back to the door.

"A name suggestion. You don't have to use it, but I think it suits you. Regardless, that's who I will refer to you as from now on, since you know we're both in my world now."

"Do I look disfigured to you?" Five asks, an eyebrow cocking up in question.

"Maybe not on the outside," Ettie replies with a shrug. Five narrows his eyes, but he leaves without another word. Once he leaves, I disable the door so that we won't be disturbed again.

"That was intense," I finally say, watching Ettie closely. "I guess I don't have to ask you how you feel about Five…"

"Scar, you should definitely call him Scar from now on."

"Scar? I'm not sure I like you naming other men, Ettie."

"Oh, please. Will you get over your possessiveness already? You're being a little insane."

"I don't think it's possible to stop being possessive over you, Sunshine," I murmur with a smile, as I pull her to her feet and take her in my arms. "How come Five gets a cool name like Scar and I'm stuck with Leo?"

"You're insane," she mumbles, but her body relaxes into my arms.

"Hey, I'm just curious."

"Leo was a king. And you wanted something besides Simba, remember," she laughs.

"Scar sounds menacing, though. It gives off a don't fuck with me vibe."

"Do you have a television here? One with streaming ability?" she asks, and I nod.

"In the bedroom," I tell her.

"Then, tonight we'll watch The Lion King and after I'll show you who Leo the Lion is."

"If we must," I respond with a long, drawn out, whining breath.

"What now?" she laughs.

"It's just I can think of other things I'd like to do to you in bed," I murmur, bending down to kiss her.

I feel her fingers tangle in my hair as our kiss deepens. My eyes are closed and I swear that it's the echo of her heart beating in my ears that I'm listening to. The sound soothes me, brings me a peace I've never known before Ettie came back into my life.

We kiss slowly, almost reverently. Taking our time and learning each other, tasting each other. It's a kiss of pleasure, but also it feels like a promise.

A promise of more to come.

"Scar is not wrong, Leo. I could bring danger to you all by being here. A relationship between us…"

"My very existence is danger, Ettie. It won't change if you're not here. What will change is the fact that I wouldn't want to live without you."

"I could add *more* danger," she argues.

"Danger is sexy," I respond, letting my thumb dance lazily back and forth against the under-swell of her breast.

"Leo, I'm trying to be serious here."

I feel a shiver run through her and I smile. "I am being serious, Ettie," I murmur softly, I lean down and brush my lips against hers again, then trail kisses along her jaw line. "I can't imagine a world where you weren't close to hold," I add, stopping to place a kiss against the shell of her ear. "To kiss." I let my teeth rake against the lobe, sucking it into my mouth. Again, I can feel my fangs begin to form, something that never happens unless I'm feeding. I fight them back, wanting to do nothing that will scare Ettie away. Instead, I nibble along the side of her neck, the artery jumping in her neck enticing me, making my cock grow even harder and push against my jeans. "To tease."

"Leo," she murmurs, so much hunger in her voice that I know if I pressed it, she'd give me more. My hand drifts up, my finger petting her hard nipple, which is pebbled and pushing against her shirt.

"To adore," I add, as she tilts her head, giving me access. Does she know what she's inviting? Does she realize how she's tempting the animal inside of me? It takes all of my self-control to beat it back. I pull back to look at her, her eyes dilated and full of yearning and desire. "Would you be able to imagine a world without me, Ettie?"

"Leo—"

"Would everything just go on like normal for you, if I wasn't with you? Or would you ache for me, and miss having me with you so much that you couldn't breathe for it?"

"Oh God, Leo, I—"

"Because that's how I'd feel if you left me, Ettie. I would grieve you with every breath I take."

"Maybe you would, but maybe that's just because you think I'm your mate," she murmurs.

"Humans don't specifically have mates as far as I know. Does that mean you wouldn't feel the same as I do if we were apart, Ettie?"

"We have soulmates," she replies.

"Isn't that the same thing, Ettie?"

"Maybe," she allows. "I'm not sure, Leo. All of this is so new to me…"

"I guess what you need to ask yourself, is if you think I'm your soulmate then, my love. Because I think you're the only one of us that is having trouble accepting that fate wants us to be together."

"How can you be so sure?"

"How can you not be?" I ask her without using my voice, instead opting to remind her of the connection we have. *"You didn't have this connection with Seven. Yet, Seven and I are physically and biologically alike. Why do you think you can talk with me like this and yet you can't with Seven, Ettie?"*

Confusion clouds her beautiful eyes, hiding her desire from me. I step away, feeling as if I've given her enough to think about—at least for now.

"Leo..."

"Think about it, Ettie. For now, get some rest, you didn't get much sleep the last couple of days. I need to meet with Four and the other Council members. Then, I'll come back and we'll have dinner together and watch this movie you spoke of."

I give her a brief kiss and then I walk out. Praying that I somehow reach her, because I wasn't lying. I don't think I could survive without Ettie in my life, but if that's what she chooses...

I would let her go...even if in doing so, means my death.

```
┌─────────────────────────────────┐
│                                 │
│              29                 │
│                                 │
│             Ettie               │
│                                 │
└─────────────────────────────────┘
```

"So in conclusion, you really, *really* don't like Five," Leo jokes, pulling me deeper into his warm body.

We're in bed together, and he's under the covers. He *is* wearing pajama bottoms, which I'm pretty sure he hates, but is wearing them because of me. His chest is bare however, and so warm that even lying my head on it makes my body tingle. After Leo left earlier, I did as he suggested and spent that time evaluating how I'd deal with not having Leo in my life again. I got used to it in our time apart, but everything is different now. Plus, there's the matter of my blood. Leo has carefully ignored my questions about how he's feeling and if he's been able to drink again. I'm pretty sure he hasn't though, because he's still very pale. Tomorrow, I'm going to have to talk with Seven and hold him to our bargain. First, I need to get through my meeting with the one they call Four. I'm nervous about that. If he's anything like Five... I might be in trouble.

"It's more like I don't trust him. I might have been able to stop him from pushing into my mind, but some of his thoughts I could read clearly. There's a darkness in him that I truly don't trust."

"It could be the animal inside of us, Ettie."

"Why do you refer to yourself like that, Leo? You say it often, as if there's someone else inside of you that you can't control. I promise you, there's no darkness in Seven or you like I felt in Five."

"That's something I guess. I don't think I could handle you being afraid of me, Ettie."

"That would never happen," I assure him. "Tell me why you keep talking about an animal inside of you."

"Well, that's kind of what it feels like. Although, it's more like an instinct to survive and kill those that put that survival in jeopardy and then…"

"Then?" I prompt him to continue, when he's silent and it feels like he isn't going to finish.

"Protect. Where you are concerned, Ettie, I have this over-whelming urge to protect you."

"That mating thing again?" I mumble, hating even the thought of some unknown force making Leo care for me and him having no control over it. It's like he's being forced into it and that's the last thing I want.

"Get that look off of your face, Ettie," he warns, his hand moving up and down on my back, his leg tangling with mine. I flatten my hand out against his chest, feeling the beat of his heart against my palm.

"I don't like the idea of some…*force* taking any choices out of your hands."

"If I'm okay with it, why can't you be, Sunshine?"

That's a really good question and I'm not sure I have an answer, but I try.

"I don't want something that's not real."

Leo leans down rubbing the side of his face against mine in the most tender, erotic move that I think I've ever experienced. Then he kisses me, the tip of his tongue teasing my lip, waiting for me to let him inside. He kisses me slowly, his tongue sliding against mine. He begins biting at my mouth, sucking on my lips and then deepening the kiss so that everything fades away, but him. I lose myself, I let go of my worries and I just feel, letting my eyes close.

I feel his hand move up my thigh, sliding under his shirt that I'm wearing. His fingers are slightly rough, teasing my skin. I want him. There's no denying that. I'm drawn to Leo in ways that I never understood when I was younger and as I got older and realized what arousal was, I knew the feelings I had for him were special. Now those feelings are even more alive, more electric and intense. One of his fingers dips into the lace waistband of my panties. My eyes instantly open and I find myself staring into Leo's intense gaze. I bite my lip because his eyes have taken on an amber color. They aren't frightening like Seven's was the day they argued. Leo's eyes are beautiful, but I think everything about Leo is beautiful. I always have.

"Let me make you feel good, Sunshine."

"There's so much unknown," I murmur, my resistance weakening even as I worry that if we do anything together it might make the bond Leo is trapped under stronger.

"I can tell you what I know, Ettie."

"What's that?"

"That I want you more than my next breath. I don't care if there's an unknown reason out there, in my book some things defy explanation. You're beautiful on the outside, but I've met beautiful women before. None of them brings me to life like you do. You're even more beautiful on the inside and that inside is what makes me feel…*satisfied.*"

"Satisfied," I murmur, feeling my lips move into a smile. "You make me sound like an expensive steak dinner, Leo."

"I can eat you up if that's what you want, Ettie," he promises darkly, taking my breath away as visions of him with his head buried between my legs come to mind. "Exactly like that," he says, his voice husky as he reminds me that he can see in my thoughts as clearly as I can see his.

"I'm not sure…," I whisper, still unable to let go of all of my fears.

"Then how about," he suggests with a smile. "I just give you a small taste of the pleasure I want to give you?" As he's talking, his fingers slip deeper into my panties and the pads of them brush against the lips of my pussy.

"A small taste might be okay," I murmur, so wet that I know he can feel it. I might be embarrassed about that, but his fingers slide in deeper and seek out my clit. After that, I forget about everything but the way Leo makes me feel.

30

Leo

I could lie here forever and watch Ettie sleep. Using my fingers to make her come, seeing the pleasure wash over her face. It's something I never thought I'd experience in my life. I never knew what I was missing before Ettie, but she's a gift. I know she thinks I have no choice in the way I feel about her because of the mating bond, but nothing could be further from the truth. There could be a room of women and it'd still be her every time.

I just don't know how to make her realize that.

Today is the day she's supposed to meet with Four. I worried about it until I saw the way she handled Five...*Scar.* Could Ettie be right about him? It's entirely possible. He's always held himself apart from the rest of us and it's clear he has some form of resentment against Four.

There's so much to think about, including the fact that Ettie's mother and Draven are still out there. I can't shake this feeling that they're trying to find Ettie even now—trying to find us. There are a few of us who believe the only way to clearly shake Draven permanently, or at least for a long time, is to blow up the lab. I just wanted my freedom, but now I wonder if that might be the only way to truly be free. I don't want those monsters coming after my Ettie.

Especially if I'm not here to protect her.

I haven't talked about it with the others yet, at least not extensively, but I'm getting weaker. I've tried to drink, even forced myself and even though I've managed to swallow it, my body rejects it. It comes back up every time. Seven is urging me to talk to Ettie, but she's already worried about the mating bond. How can I confess that I need her blood to survive? She overhead parts of my conversation with Seven, I'm just thankful she seems clueless about the blood bond. If she realized that the bond was the reason I'm having trouble digesting other blood? She'd be more convinced than ever that I don't care for her. In her mind, it's all some kind of magical spell and there's no emotion. Nothing could be further from the truth. I love Ettie. I've always loved her, but now it's all different. Now, she's an adult and I want her in every way imaginable.

Now, I can't imagine my life without her.

Which means I need to find a way around this. I need to fix this. I have a miracle in Ettie and it might be all new to me and to others, but I instinctively know that this is how it's meant to be. Ettie is my destiny, my reason for being here. I won't give her up without a fight.

With the decision renewed, I rise up quietly from the bed, careful not to wake her. I can't resist looking back at her once more, her dark curls falling loosely on her pillow around her like a beautiful crown. God, she's beautiful. I need her soon. Last night was all about her, bringing her pleasure, getting her used to being with me, but soon…

I shake my head. I can't think about that right now. Hell, my balls are already so sore it's painful to walk. I move to the bathroom, get dressed quickly and clean up. If I hurry, I can meet with Four and the others in the lab before Ettie even wakes. Six is a genius—quite literally—when it comes to the lab. He instinctively knows things and he loves running tests and figuring things out. This will give him just one more thing to figure out. He'll find the answer, he has to. Six is also training Seven. Between the three of us, surely, we can come up with a solution. Christ, all these numbers. Ettie is right, we need real names. It's time to leave our past behind us.

I lean down and place a kiss on Ettie's forehead, looking down at the woman I love. Maybe there is something to this whole soulmate thing, because it certainly feels like she lives inside of mine.

"Leo," Ettie mumbles in her sleep, and emotion so strong it squeezes in my chest, to the point it's almost painful how good it feels. I have to find an answer. I can't let Ettie know about the blood bond. I won't allow her to see me as a parasite that needs to feed off her to survive. I can't.

I walk into the other room and just as I get to the door, a wave of dizziness swamps me. It's so intense that my knees buckle, forcing me to hold onto the wall for support. It takes a good ten minutes before I get control again. I'm thankful Ettie wasn't around to see that. I close my eyes as my heart slows back down and I'm able to breathe easy again. Then, I head straight to the lab. I need answers and I need them fast.

I'm running out of time…

31

Ettie

"Where's Leo?" I ask Seven, worried.

He was gone when I got up this morning and other than a text telling me he was held up on business, I've not heard from him. I'm about to meet Four and I really, *really*, wanted Leo with me. Instead, it was Seven who showed up at my door to escort me to the lab. With each step we take, I get more and more nervous.

"Four sent him on some errands."

"Seven, why do I get the feeling you're not telling me everything?"

"Because you're crazy?"

"I am not."

"Little One, you ran away to live in a mostly underground bunker with seven creatures who live off of human blood. You are definitely crazy."

"It's not like you and Leo gave me much choice," I mumble. "I need to talk to you about Leo. We need to discuss how to make him drink—"

"After you meet with Four. Let's tackle one issue at a time, shall we?"

"I guess, but you're not getting out of our deal, Seven."

"I promise, I want Leo healthy as much as you do."

"Okay," I mumble ungraciously.

"I do have something I've been wanting to talk to you about. From now on, you should call me Stark."

"Stark?" I ask, with a small giggle.

"My new name. Do you like it?"

"Did you name yourself after the Iron Man?"

"It's badass, right?"

"I guess. I mean you could have picked worse I guess."

"I did almost go with Thor," Seven admits as the door to the lab opens.

"You wanted to name yourself after a god?"

"Well more so because he packs a large hammer," Seven says with a wink. I refuse to blush, instead I roll my eyes at him.

"You're right, Stark fits. You definitely have the ego."

"Words hurt Esther," Seven laughs. "Besides, I figure I needed to take things into my own hands. If I didn't, you'd probably name me Mufasa. Leo warned me about your love of Lion names."

"Mufasa is a beautiful name and I loved him," I defend, still giggling.

"It's a great name, but I don't even know how to spell that shit. Stark is simple and to the point."

"Whatever, *Stark*. As long as you're not a number, I can deal."

"Do you have a name for me, Esther Lane?"

All humor leaves me as a booming voice that sounds like it echoes in the room surrounds me. I look for the source and there's this huge—*freaking huge*—man standing against the wall. He's dressed in all black, his skin dark, and his hair black, but shaved short on his head. He has a beard, which is also trimmed short and has traces of gray. The black cable-knit sweater he's wearing stretches over his muscles and he's intimidating to say the least.

"Do you want a name?" I ask, cautiously. I take a few more steps, but don't go too far into the room.

"I believe I do. I heard you already named Five. I'm not sure he's happy with it, however."

"I'm positive there's not much *Scar* is happy with."

"I'm told you have the gift of insight. It can be a heavy cross."

"Insight? I never thought of it that way, I guess."

"You must be talented if you read into *Scar's* mind. He keeps it hidden from me, he has a formidable power of his own."

I try to reach out and read Four's mind, but I can't. It's like there's a wall up.

"Maybe I don't, because I can't read you," I tell him, stopping my efforts, because it's impossible.

"I'm old and one of my skills is to block myself off from everyone."

"Scar doesn't have that talent?" I ask, genuinely interested.

"He does, but it's harder to put up our guards when emotion is involved. Scar has a lot of…"

"Hate," I finish for him.

"Unfortunately, yes. That's not what you truly want to talk about though, is it, Esther?"

"You've been in my mind, you tell me."

"You felt me there?" he asks.

"I *allowed* you there," I qualify. I'm kind of bluffing. Four is very powerful, it emanates off of him in waves. I don't honestly know if I could keep him out of my head, but I don't mind him thinking that I can.

For some reason, he laughs. Shit…I felt him pull away, but maybe he didn't. Maybe he's hearing my thoughts right now and I'm making a fool of myself. I decide to ignore it and soldier on.

"You're concerned about Leo," Four says, cutting away everything else and leaving us with the main worry that I have.

"No, I'm not," I answer.

Four frowns, confused.

"I'm terrified for him. He doesn't want to admit to me that he has to have my blood and he is getting weaker. I can see it, even when he tries to hide it from me. Last night, I could sense his worry even while we were together. He does a good job of not worrying around me so that the emotions don't show...but they're there."

"He hasn't figured out yet that you can read his worries, even if he doesn't voice them to you?"

"I believe he thinks if he concentrates on me and the emotions he has for me, the rest won't come through and for the most part, he's right..."

"Except when he is not," Four finishes and I nod in agreement.

"Most humans in my experience do not like the idea of being a...shall we call it a living donor?" he says, moving with such grace that I can't help but stare as he moves into a chair. He's almost poetry in motion. It's unnerving.

"I'd give Leo anything so he could live. It doesn't bother me."

"And yet, you want to know how to break the blood bond. You could see how this would confuse an old man."

"How old are you?"

"Older than you can imagine, Esther," he replies and I blink. Since he was made in the lab like Leo, I don't see how that's possible, but that's a puzzle for another time.

"I only wish to break the blood bond, because I don't want Leo forced to be with me against his will."

"You think the blood bond makes us act against our will?"

"I think it can," I qualify. "I want Leo to have the right to choose, not be trapped with me because he licked a drop of blood without thinking."

"I'm positive he was thinking very clearly, Esther. I can smell your life's blood from here." I jerk in response to his answer, unnerved and more than a little weirded out. "Your scent is delicious."

"Are you trying to scare me?"

"Not at all. If I were, you would know. If you intend on living here with all of us, you should get used to the fact that we are more like animals than men most of the time. Let us get on with it, I've been in the light too long. When you get to my age, without proper sustenance, it can wear on you. You wish to know how to break the bond that has been forged with Leo. Yes?"

"So it's true vampires can't go out into the light? Oh, and yes, definitely, yes."

Four's lips curl in distaste. "Old wives tales always have kernels of the truth in them. We can discuss that at a later time. I'm afraid you won't like either of my answers, Esther."

"Are you going to tell me it can't be done?" I ask him.

"No. On the contrary, it can be done and has before."

"Then, tell me how."

"Well, we can hook Leo up to a machine to keep him alive and then pump out all of his blood while flowing new in. Think of it as a transfusion on a much larger scale. It can be dangerous, there's a chance he could die, but I know of one case where it has been successful. Of course, that subject died later on, but that's neither here nor there, I suppose."

"That sounds too dangerous. What's the second option?"

"I don't suppose you would take my word for it that blood bonds don't override free will?"

"What's the second option?" I press, ignoring his question. There's no way I could trust he is telling me the truth. I want to be with Leo, but I want him to be with me because he cares about me—not because he has no other choice.

"I didn't think so. Did you hear that, Luciana? They don't listen. I don't know why I expect them to, they never do. Then again, you never did either, did you, my love?" I blink as Four apparently starts talking to someone else…someone not in the room. "Yes, I suppose I should. I am getting tired."

He rises from the chair and walks toward the door. Again, I am drawn to his movements, because it's almost as if he is floating as he walks.

"Wait, tell me the second way to break the blood bond," I urge him. Seven comes to my side and puts his arm on me.

"Hush, do not upset him. Sometimes he gets tired, and his thoughts are erratic. He will be back."

"But, Leo…," I murmur, the words sounding mournful.

Four surprises both of us by turning back around and when he looks at me his eyes are clear. I get the feeling Seven is wrong, I don't think there's anything wrong with Four. In fact, I think there is more going on than what we can see. And for a moment, I feel him searching my brain again. He's reading my mind again, sifting through my thoughts and I let him read all of them.

"Why would you call me Oracle?" he asks.

I hadn't even realized that out of all of my stray thoughts he'd pick up on that one. "Because you're wise and have answers, even when we don't want to hear them. Plus, I kind of like you, but I'm not sure I should. It's from a movie. The Matrix, you should watch it."

"You watch a lot of movies, Esther."

"I was alone most of my life. Movies and reading were my comforts."

Four nods and then smiles. "I shall accept the name. It will be the only one I answer to from here on."

"Will you answer my question?" I ask, before he can get the chance to leave again.

"It's quite simple, Esther. The only other way to break the bond is for you to die," he states and then he turns back around, the door opens and before he steps out, he looks at me over my shoulder. "I do hope you don't choose that one. I have a feeling Luciana and I will like you."

I stare after him, long after the door closes.

"Who is Luciana?" I ask Seven.

"No one knows."

"Interesting," I murmur. Then I pull my thoughts to the one thing I can control. "So, how are we going to get Leo to agree to have his blood drained?" I ask Seven and he looks at me like I'm crazy.

Heck, I'm starting to think I might be...

"Leo?" Ettie whispers sleepily, as I slide into bed with her.

"Were you expecting someone else?" I joke, pulling her into my body and spooning her. I kiss the side of her neck, my eyes closing at the pleasure and relief I feel having her close to me once again. I don't wear clothes to bed. Since giving her an orgasm and watching her eyes as she came while I used my hand on her, I don't want clothes between us in bed. She's wearing my shirt, and perversely I'm okay with that, even if I'd rather have her naked. When she's wearing my shirt it's like my stamp of ownership on her and fuck if I don't like that, too.

"You've been gone all day," Ettie responds. She turns to her back, stretching out to turn the bedside light on. It's not very big, so it mostly just bathes our small area in soft light. She looks up at me, worry etched on her face.

"I had some things to do."

"Out of the blue? You were supposed to go with me to meet Oracle."

"The *what*?"

"Four. His name is Oracle now."

"You named Four?"

She shrugs in reply. "Where have you been?"

126

"I told you, Sunshine. I had some errands to do."

"You were out trying to drink."

"Ettie—"

"You weren't able to, were you, Leo?"

"I'm fine, Ettie. There's nothing for you to worry about."

"Will you stop lying to me?"

"I'm not," I growl, sitting up so I can look down at her. "I'm tired, let's go to bed and we'll talk about this in the morning."

"You're tired because you're starving."

"They'll figure out what's wrong with me soon, Ettie."

"But, you already know what's wrong, Leo. You tasted my blood and this damn blood bond is making you act irrationally and it's starving you to death."

"I'm going to kill Seven," I growl, getting out of bed and reaching down on the floor to find my pants.

"It wasn't Seven that told me, Leo. I overheard all of your conversation, not just the part about you not being able to drink. I can also read your thoughts and feel your worry. You seem to forget that," Ettie responds, standing up on the opposite side of the bed, folding her arms at her chest.

"Damn it, Ettie," I growl, feeling cornered. "I'm dealing with this."

"But, you aren't. You're pale, you're losing weight and—"

"And I'll fix it. This is not your fault. You didn't tell me to lick the blood on the back of your neck. That was all me. I'll fix this. It doesn't concern you."

"It doesn't concern me?!?!"

"Ettie—"

"Well, that's just proof, isn't it?"

"Proof of what?" I ask, exasperated.

"That you don't truly care for me. It's the blood bond guiding your actions."

"That's bullshit and you know it, Ettie."

"You don't even think the fact that you're killing yourself is any of my business. That doesn't sound like you care about me at all, Leo."

"Damn it, Ettie, I love you."

"As a friend, maybe," she replies and I can't believe she has the nerve to say that to me.

"Did it feel like I was interested in just being a friend last night when my hand was between your legs and you were crying out my name, Ettie?" I growl, so frustrated that I can't see straight. She has no idea the depth of emotion I feel for her.

"That's just sex, that's not a relationship, Leo."

"How in the hell do you know? You've never been in a relationship before." Frustration is pushing me to the edge. I should handle Ettie with care, but damn it, this is so frustrating and I don't have any damn answers, other than I love her and there's not some big force making me feel that way.

I just do.

"Well, neither have you," she huffs.

"I'm starting to think that was self-preservation on my part," I growl.

I can see that what I said hits her hard. It's all over her face, but more than that, I can feel the hurt inside of her well up and instantly my anger is gone. I feel like an ass.

"That's exactly what I mean."

"Ettie…"

"You're in luck, Leo. Oracle told me how to break the blood bond between us. That way you can go back to the way things were before and I can just…leave."

"No. Absolutely not."

"What? Are you crazy?"

"Maybe I am. I don't know anymore, Ettie. What I do know is that I love our connection and it makes me feel whole for the first time in my life. I'm not giving that up."

"I don't know what to do, Leo. You can't starve yourself to death. You have to use me then."

"I don't want you to see me as some kind of leech that

uses you to survive, Ettie, and that's your biggest worry. I can tell you that it's not like that, but we both know you won't take my word for it. Just think about it, do you honestly believe that in the years we've been apart if what you and I have wasn't special, that I wouldn't have had a reaction to any of the blood I've drank before you?" I ask her, dropping my pants back on the floor, hoping like hell I can make her understand.

"Maybe it's because I was there? Or it was fresh?" she questions hopelessly.

I take her in my arms and sit down on the bed with Ettie in my lap. I curl my hand against the side of her neck, my thumb brushing back and forth on her cheek, as I hold her face so that I can look into her eyes.

"I'm going to enjoy killing your mother for making you feel that you aren't enough. Ettie, you're everything to me. You're special. I know in my fucking soul that this connection is because it's *you* and *me*. That's it, Sunshine, nothing else. Maybe I'm not a normal man, but you need to understand that I am your man. *Yours.*"

Small tears gather in the corner of her eyes, and I move my hand down to swipe them away.

"I love you, Leo."

I smile, the words sliding inside of me and taking root.

"I love you, Ettie."

"You have to drink from me, if this is us, then that's part of us, too."

"Then you will never know if my feelings are real. I think I understand it's because of the shit your mother put in your head over the years, but I don't want you to question my love. I don't want you to doubt your worth in our life together, Ettie."

"I'll give you three more days, and then you have to agree to drink. I can't lose you, Leo."

I sigh, and study her face and then I give in. I don't know how to find the answers she needs in three days…

"Three days," I agree and I'm rewarded with a soft smile pulling at her lips that blurs when she leans up and kisses me.

I lay back on the bed, Ettie stretching out over me, the kiss deepening.

"Sunshine," I groan.

She pulls away to look down at me, her dark eyes glimmering with desire, her lips swollen from our kiss. My hand is on her neck, her hair spilling around her face.

"Damn, you're beautiful, Ettie."

I don't even realize that I'm using my mind to talk to her, but I know she hears me when the smile deepens on her lips.

"Make love to me, Leo."

Her words are still vibrating through me when she leans down and I take her lips again. This is my woman.

My life.

My world.

```
┌─────────────────────────────┐
│                             │
│            33               │
│                             │
│           Ettie             │
│                             │
└─────────────────────────────┘
```

"Are you sure, Ettie?" Leo asks when we break apart.

"I want this, Leo. I want you."

Our eyes stay locked, as his hand moves slowly up my thigh, sliding centimeter by centimeter under his shirt that I'm wearing to sleep in. My breath feels heavy in my chest, and I audibly swallow, this moment feeling like the most important of my life.

"My beautiful, Ettie," he whispers, his voice soft, tender and full of emotion. I've never felt beautiful in my life, but with Leo looking down at me like he is right now, I feel like Cinderella finally getting her happily ever after.

"Leo," I gasp, as his hand slides against the rounded globe of my ass, squeezing it and his fingers drifting into the cleft, teasing me.

"No panties," he grins, a smile so deep it lights his eyes. I bite my lip as his fingers explore my ass. A breath shudders through me as wetness pools between my legs, painting the inside of my thighs.

"There didn't seem to be a reason to wear them," I admit. "I know what I want."

"Let me hear you say it, Sunshine," he says, his fingers moving against the tight ring of muscles at my ass, not going inside, merely teasing me, tantalizing me as thoughts of what he could and might do to me fire through my brain and I can barely breathe while I wait. I'm completely at his mercy.

"You, Leo. I want you."

"There's no going back, Ettie. Whatever happens, this is us. I pledge myself to you, Sunshine, forever."

"Leo—"

"Forever, Ettie."

"Love me, Leo," I whisper, refusing to let my doubts ruin this moment for either of us.

"We need to go slow, Baby. The last thing I want to do is hurt you. This is all new for you," he murmurs and I smile, my bottom lip rubbing against my teeth as I look into his eyes, blushing.

"It's new for you too, Leo"

"Yeah, Baby, it is, but I'm pretty sure it's going to be good for me no matter what happens."

"It will be for me too, Leo."

"Ettie."

"It will be, Leo. It has to because it's you. I've loved you my whole life."

"My sweet, Ettie," Leo groans and his fingers tighten in my hair until it's almost painful and he pulls my lips to his, kissing me with such hunger my body feels as if it's on fire. He owns my mouth, claiming it, our tongues tangling in an erotic dance that somehow mirrors what I know is coming soon.

I feel his cock pushing against my center, rubbing against me, stretching...growing. Leo's not small, and I wonder how he's going to fit inside of me. I should be nervous, I suppose, but that's impossible with Leo. With Leo, I'm safe. I feel hot all over, and I know Leo realizes how wet I am. He can't help it, because as I rub against his hard cock, I know I'm making him wet. His hand moves from my ass to my hip and he holds me still as we break apart.

"Enough of that sweet, Ettie. You rub against me much

more like that and I'm going to come before I get inside of you."

"It feels good," I explain, self-consciously.

"I know, Baby, but it's about to feel a hell of a lot better."

"Hurry," I urge him and he lets out a soft chuckle.

"Not on your life, Ettie. I want to take my time with you."

"Do that next time," I urge him and his hold in my hair tightens and he kisses my lips hard and quick.

"Stop being cute," he mutters, as he moves me so I'm sitting on him, looking down. My hands are on his abdomen, steadying me as he stares up at me. He puts his hands at the top button of the shirt I'm wearing and his gaze never leaves mine as he undoes it, then, the next… *and the next.*

It's deliciously slow. It's torture, and yet, every button is like this huge build up, ramping up my excitement and hunger for him. When the shirt is completely undone, I can feel the cool air against the skin of my stomach. My nipples harden even more, as the fabric of the shirt brushes against them and I take a deep breath, my body trembling. A new wave of wetness gathers and I close my eyes as I feel it covering his hard shaft that has pushed between the lips of my pussy and is pressing against my throbbing clit.

"Are you with me, Ettie?" Leo asks, his voice unbelievably soft and sweet.

"Oh, yeah."

"Open your eyes, Sunshine." I do as he asks, rewarded at the love shining in his. Surely that can't help but be real. I can almost physically feel it. "That's my girl. I want to look into your eyes when I finally make you mine, Ettie." He pulls my shirt apart, exposing me completely to him. I help take it off and he drops it over the side of the bed. My hands come up on reflex, trying to shield my breasts from him and I can feel myself flush, even though my whole body feels as if it's on fire. "No, Baby. Don't cover yourself from me. You're safe with me, Ettie. You always will be."

"This is kind of new for me," I remind him, licking my lips.

"Me too, remember?"

"Yeah," I answer so softly that I'm not sure he can hear me. His hands come up to circle each of my wrists as he brings them down. My body jerks, as his fingers accidentally brush against my swollen nipples.

"Are you tender there, Ettie?" he murmurs, his fingers coming back up to swipe against them.

"Yes."

"Can I kiss you there?" he asks and my eyes go large and round as surprise hits me. I nod my head yes, overcoming my shyness because I want Leo to do anything he wants to me.

I'm his.

He stretches toward me, placing the sweetest kiss on my nipple that sends goosebumps all over my body. I sway into him, needing more, even though I'm not sure what it is I want. Then, Leo moves his tongue over the nipple as his fingers come up to play with the other one and I know immediately what I want.

More.

My fingers push into his hair as I hold his head to me, my eyes closing as the sensations swarm me. He sucks, licks, and kisses my nipple, all while I rock against his cock. I'm so close to coming, I can feel it and God, I want it. When I feel Leo's teeth bite my nipple, I hold my breath, wondering if he'll penetrate the skin and take my blood. I'm scared of what this bond could mean and if it will keep him from choosing freely, but at the same time...I want him to take my blood like this more than I've ever wanted anything else in my life.

He doesn't though. All too soon, he pulls away and the cool air hits my wet nipple, as he pinches the other one.

"Rise up, Ettie. Rest on your knees," he growls, and now I can hear the hunger in his voice and it's beautiful. I immediately find his gaze, his eyes amber in color, burning with an intensity that makes my heart beat even faster. I do exactly what he asks, knowing that this is it. After all of these years, I will finally belong to Leo. It's what I always dreamed of, even before I knew what that meant. "Reach between us and wrap your hand around my cock, Sunshine, and guide me inside of you." As my hand encircles him, holding his wet cock tightly, Leo's eyes close and his body shudders. I stop, wondering if I've done something wrong. When his eyes open this time, there's a flare of heat radiating in them that almost hypnotizes me because it's so potent. "Keep going, Ettie," he urges, his voice so graveled in texture that it almost doesn't sound like him.

I lick my lips nervously, still keeping my gaze locked on his. I position him at my entrance, holding him there. Leo's hands go to my hips, his fingers biting into my skin.

"Leo?" I question, when he doesn't make a move, just staring into my eyes.

"Take me inside, Baby. Just a little."

I breathe an almost silent sigh of relief. I slide down on his cock until the head breaches me and he's pressing against proof of my virginity. He stops me before I can take him deeper. I want him, I'm so ready and I'm so drenched that I'm more than wet enough for what comes next. I might be a virgin, but this is Leo and I know this is right.

"Leo, please." I don't even care that I'm begging. This is too slow. It's killing me.

"Mine," he growls. "All mine."

With those words, he pushes inside of me so quickly that I lose my breath from the swiftness of it. There's pain as he tears through my virginity, but it's nothing compared to the pleasure that immediately courses through me when he stretches me, claiming me, bringing us together in a way that I know I'll never be with anyone else. I belong to Leo, I know it, and when I look into his eyes as I ride him, bringing us both to our climax, I begin to believe that Leo belongs to me, too.

His hand reaches out and grabs mine. Our fingers curl into each other and we hold on tightly as our eyes stay locked on one another, and I ride him harder and faster. It's beautiful.

My orgasm builds quickly and just before I fall over the edge, taking him with me, I reach out to him with my mind.

"I love you, Leo."

"I love you, Ettie. I'll always love you."

Those words sound like a vow as he takes my mouth, kissing me, swallowing down my cries of completion, while he comes deep inside of me.

Perfection.

"You're killing yourself."

"I refuse to listen to anyone that names himself after a comic book hero," I mumble.

"Stark is an awesome name. It sure as hell is better than a lion who won't eat meat."

"What are you talking about?"

"Leo the Lion. Don't you watch Netflix?"

"Net what?"

"God, you're such a moron."

"Takes one to know one, *Stark.*"

"See? That name will make women drop their panties, go to their knees and worship my dick."

"There's just one problem with that, asshole."

"What's that?"

"If you can't find a woman who makes you react like my Ettie does to me, your cock is as useless as that brain you have in your head."

Seven frowns at me, and rubs the back of his head. "I've been thinking about that. If it happened to you, and from what Oracle says, happens with others of our kind, then my only solution is to start dating and find my Ettie."

"Ettie's aren't easy to find," I warn him, smiling as I think of my woman.

"God, will you take pity on me and wipe that smile off your face?"

"I feel like smiling," I laugh.

"I would, too, if I was having sex every night. I've had to give up watching porn, it's boring as hell and just makes the emptiness worse."

"It's much better in person than watching anyway."

"I could hate you," he mutters and I laugh out loud. "Bastard. In all seriousness, though, I'm happy for you."

"Thanks, Sev—Stark. That name is going to take some getting used to."

"You need to break down and drink from Ettie. I know for a fact she's offered. Stop starving yourself. Hell, you look like death warmed over. I'm not sure how much longer you can survive like this."

"You're starting to sound like Ettie," I mumble.

"She's talking sense. Not to mention she gave you three days, it's been seven. I don't know if you realize this or not, but Ettie is not very patient. She's going to take matters into her own hands soon and then you're going to have a hell of a mess, Leo."

"There's nothing she can do."

"If you truly think that, then you don't realize that her and Oracle have struck up quite the friendship. She's with him almost every day."

I tap down the jealousy that makes me feel. I know Ettie wouldn't ever betray me. I don't think Four would do that to me either. I can't deny however, that I don't like the idea of Ettie spending time with a man who is not me.

"I've had to sleep some through the day," I mumble. "But, I think I'm getting closer. I actually held some down for a good ten minutes today."

"Ten minutes? Oh wow, you're so cured now. We can all quit worrying."

"Will you shut up? It's progress."

"It's shit and we both know it. You can't keep going like this."

"Did you walk all the way down here, just to bust my balls?" I mutter. I'm in the weight room, down two flights from mine and Ettie's room. Four—or Oracle, as everyone has begun calling him—seems to find comfort in the darkness and being further underground. I always thought it was weird, but now, I hide out here. I even sleep on the sofa in the small room to the side some during the day. It helps me hide just how bad going without blood is from Ettie…well, mostly. Seven's right. She's not happy with me and we've argued over it the last couple of days, especially after her three-day deadline passed.

"I'm worried about you, Leo. Hell, we all are."

"If I don't get anywhere tonight, I'll talk with Ettie tomorrow. I just don't want her thinking I'm only with her because of the blood. She already feels like she's not worth anything thanks to that evil bitch of a mother she lived with."

"I meant to talk to you about that."

"What?" I ask, warning signals instantly firing inside my brain.

"I can't be sure. But there seems to be a lot more movement from Draven's headquarters. You know Four had set up a surveillance there. The company we hired out has seen a lot of helicopters and transport there the last two weeks."

"Do we know where they're going, or hell, anything about it?"

"Not yet, but at least two of the helicopters landed in Arizona and another one landed in Arkansas."

"You think they're trying to find us? Searching the path we took to get Ettie here?"

"Can't be sure, but I'd almost bet money on it."

"Fuck."

"Pretty much. That means we may be in for a fight. You need to be healthy, Leo—sooner rather than later, Man. Get your shit together."

"I'll talk with her tomorrow," I repeat. "I need to try at least one more time."

Seven...*Stark* shakes his head, but he leaves me in peace and for now, that's enough. I close my eyes, hoping to sleep a couple more hours before I try the next round of blood. I'm praying for a miracle, but I'm pretty sure it's not going to happen.

35

Ettie

Leo was still sleeping when I left our room this morning. It wasn't normal sleep either, it was so deep that I was afraid he wasn't breathing. I had to put my ear down on his heart just to make sure I could hear it beating. Then, because even that was faint, I stared for ten minutes to make sure his chest was moving to indicate he was breathing. It's not that it took ten minutes but the movement was so slight that even after I thought I saw it, I was scared I imagined it and had to keep looking.

I'm driving myself insane. This needs to be fixed and if Leo is too stubborn to do it then I'm going to. Of course, I'd love it if I knew beyond a shadow of a doubt that Leo was with me for some other reason than a bond he has no control over. But, I'm not willing to watch him die while he tries to find proof. Oracle mentioned the blood bond not overriding free will and if this fails, then I'm just going to have to force myself to believe that.

When I get to the lab, Seven—Stark's—head jerks up, giving me a resigned look.

"Now, how did I know you would show up this morning?" he mumbles.

"The same way I knew you'd be here trying to find an answer for Leo. Have you yet?"

"Yep. He's going to have to drink from you."

"That's about what I've decided, too. We may have to force him to," I respond with a sigh, starting to feel defeated.

"Listen, I like you and all. You're kind of like a pesky little sister, but I'm not really wanting to get into yours and Leo's kinky bedroom games."

"Not funny."

"It's kind of funny," he says, with a smile and a shrug.

"Leo won't drink willingly, Seven, and I'm not about to let him die."

"You do know he's as strong as any of us, it's not like we'll be able to force him to drink," Seven mutters, shaking his head.

"He's weak from not drinking, you said that yourself."

"Weak yes, but he's still damn powerful."

"Surely, not as powerful as a man cocky enough to name himself after a god. Right, Thor?"

"I went with Stark." I roll my eyes, and *Stark* lets out a muffled growl.

"It'd be easier if we could find a way to make him drink willingly. I'm betting if you stab yourself so it drips down your body, he won't be able to resist."

"I've tried that—yesterday, in fact," I tell him, because I did and Leo left the room like I had contracted the plague and I didn't see him the rest of the day. He must have come back later that night, however, because I woke up with him in my bed.

"Then, you didn't do it right," he says.

"There's a right way? Sorry I didn't have the handbook. I'm kind of new to all of this," I mumble, flopping down in a chair.

"You needed to be naked. Were you naked, Ettie?" he asks his question while silently laughing, his eyebrows moving up and down.

"Pervert," I laugh.

"What the fuck is going on here," Leo growls and we both

look up at Leo. He's pale and I could swear he sways a little as he storms over toward us, but he's pissed. In fact, he's so mad that the anger feels like a physical presence in the room.

"Cool your jets, Leo," Stark mumbles.

"It's getting easier to call you Stark, because you're kind of a jackass," I mutter, getting up and going over to Leo. He immediately takes me in his arms, situating his body between me and Stark.

"Do you want to tell me why I get out of bed and find you talking with my woman and asking her about being naked?" Leo demands, his voice dark and scary.

"Will you stop?" I huff, tired of this crap. I slap him on the shoulder and move away from him. "We're trying to find a way to keep you alive."

"I'm fine."

"Bullshit," Stark and I say at the same time.

"Fine. Have you found a solution?" Leo asks, sounding even more tired than he looks.

"You have to drink from me."

"Not happening. I won't become a damn albatross around your neck that you keep around so I won't die and I won't have you worrying if I'm only with you for one thing."

"God, you two are giving me a headache. It's too early for this shit."

"Fine," I respond, stepping away from him. I breathe out slowly, trying to rid my body of the frustration and the nervousness I feel. It doesn't help, but at least I tried. "Then, there's only one solution," I state calmly.

"What's that?" They both ask, looking at me expectantly. I stare at them for a moment and then take the plunge.

"Seven...," I mumble, under my breath, catching myself. This renaming business is annoying. "*Stark* is going to have to drink from me."

"You're out of your fucking mind," both of them yell so loud that I wince. Geez, you'd think I had a disease in my blood that would cause they're cocks to fall off or something. A girl could get her feelings hurt. I narrow my eyes at both of them and cross my arms at my chest in a stance that I hope tells them I'm serious. The problem is they are looking at me like they might want to strangle me.

This isn't going to go smoothly. Damn it!

36

Leo

"This is the only way to figure things out. I'm not going to let you die, and you won't take my blood until you can prove to me the bond isn't influencing you. It's the perfect solution," Ettie says, sounding so logical that part of me wants to strangle her. The thought of anyone touching her, let alone drinking from her, makes me want to kill them. I'm not sure I can keep from it if Seven—Stark, *whoever*, tries.

"I refuse," Seven responds, possibly saving his life. "Leo, do something with your woman!"

"I'm thinking of taking her back to our room and spanking her ass," I threaten.

Ettie's cheeks deepen in color as she stares at me, her eyes shooting me evil glares.

"In your dreams," she huffs at me and I shrug, she's not exactly wrong about that. I'll make her like it, too. "And I don't see why you're being such an ass, Stark. It's not like my blood can taste any worse than those bags you down." She looks at Stark as she says that and she is clearly upset at the thought he thinks she'd taste bad. I really might have to spank her ass and leave it red enough that she can't sit down comfortably for a week.

"Ettie, I'm sure you taste great." I growl at him under my breath. He holds his hand out as if to tell me to stop. "But, you belong to Leo, I'd rather not have to kill him just to survive."

"You could try," I mutter and Seven rolls his eyes at me, but then, he doesn't realize the emotions I have when it comes to Ettie. I like him, I think of him as a brother, but I could easily rip his head from his shoulders for touching Ettie and not blink. It wouldn't even take much energy because the aggression inside of me is that strong when it comes to my claim on Ettie.

"Leo is going to let you do this."

"The hell I am," I growl, looking at her as she moves away to stand in the middle of both of us.

"You idiot," she mutters. "Can't you see this is the only way to tell if you're drawn to me because of the bond, or if it's just me you want."

"It's you I *love*, Ettie. I already know that. You're the one that is questioning it, not me. Let's get that clear."

"Fine, then just drink from me already."

"No. I'm not going to be a parasite you keep around because you don't want me to die."

"The correct term is leech, I believe," Four responds, appearing out of nowhere. Ettie walks straight to him and stands beside him. My eyes narrow. Maybe their friendship has grown a little too much.

"Stand down, Young One," Four dismisses and I blink. "And my name is Oracle now," he adds, making a waving motion without even looking at me. I knew Four could read thoughts, but apparently, he can see what we're thinking as well. I sigh, rubbing my forehead. Shit is way too complicated.

"Leech?"

"Yes, Stark, believe it or not, people used to think of us as nothing more than blood suckers."

"Used to?" I ask. "You act like we've been walking among the humans for years."

"Centuries, Leo. You have no idea of our history. Your

perception is distorted thanks to Draven, but what we were and what we are now, is not always who we have been."

"You're speaking in circles, Fo—" I stop, catching myself. "Oracle."

"Now you see why I gave him that name," Ettie murmurs, but I have no idea what she's talking about. As far as I'm concerned, she's speaking in as many riddles as Four is.

"Someone condense the issues for an old man."

"Ettie wants me to drink her blood and if I don't get hooked on her, then they'll know it's not the bond causing Leo's dick to get hard."

"Jesus, I think I hate you, Stark," Ettie mutters, blushing.

"Join the crowd," I add, flipping him off and making him laugh.

"Luciana and I like this plan. You may continue."

"No way in hell," I growl, feeling my fangs elongate.

"Fuck, no," Seven adds.

"Why not?" Four responds. "It seems perfectly logical."

"Thank you," Ettie beams and Four pats her on the head.

"It's a very well thought out plan, for a confused little human."

"I...what does that mean?" Ettie questions. Four ignores her.

"I'll tell you why not, what if I get as hooked on Ettie as Leo is? Then she'll have two of us to feed all the time."

"No she won't, because if you touch her, I'll tear your head off your body."

"You won't have the same reaction," Four says, and I think this is the first time I've seen him smile.

"How can I be sure?"

"In all of my years, I've never seen the blood bond happen with two of us for the same female. You're safe, Stark. Have a drink and let's end this chaos."

"No," I growl. "I won't allow Ettie to do this."

"You what?" she asks, and I swear in that moment, I can see sparks shooting out of her eyes.

"I refuse to let you do this."

"I'm a grown woman and the last time I looked, Leo, I didn't need your permission to do anything."

"Maybe not, but if Seven so much as lays a finger on you, I'll cut it off," I respond and it's not an idle threat.

"He won't have to touch her," Four says. "We'll do this the civilized way. Ettie sit on the examining table. I'll draw the blood myself."

"Damn it, I said no."

"Good thing none of us are listening then," Four replies. "Honestly, the girl is not wrong, you're killing yourself for no reason. I don't understand young people today. You get a gift, you think you would embrace it and not question it," he says shaking his head in disgust. "Now, let us get this over with. I need my rest and it's time for Luciana's meditation."

I look over at Ettie and she just shrugs. None of us know who Luciana is but Four always talks to her as if she's real and most of the time as if she's in the room with us. I snarl when I watch him draw out a small vial of Ettie's blood. I nearly sway as a wave of hunger so strong rocks through me, causing my knees to weaken. I feel my fangs press over my other teeth and I use all the self-control I have to calm down.

"Here you go," Four says, carelessly tossing the vial to Seven.

Seven looks at it and then glances over at me.

"You're sure I won't end up like Leo?" he asks Four.

"Positive. It never happens," Four answers.

Seven takes off the stopper and tilts the vial up to drink it. I make my hands into fists to keep from stopping him.

"Please calm down, Leo. It's going to be fine. You will see."

I don't respond to Ettie's voice in my head. I couldn't right now if I wanted to.

"Well, okay. It did happen once, I suppose you are right, Luciana, but they weren't our kind. They truly are animals. You remember when you tried to take one as a pet? I had him made into a rug. Those were some good times," Four rattles on.

"Wait, you mean it has happened?" I growl, my heartbeat speeding up.

"Many moons ago and with mongrels, not our breed specifically," Four waves me off like I'm worrying for nothing. Meanwhile, Seven has finished the blood.

"Well?" Ettie asks.

Seven looks at her and frowns. "Well, what?"

"Don't be an asshole, you know what I'm asking."

"You mean do I want to drink more of your blood and bow at your feet and beg you to pick me over Leo?"

"Seven," I warn him, my voice vibrating with anger. "Did it change you?" I ask, not wanting to know, but desperate at the same time.

"Are you asking if my dick is hard, Leo?"

"I'm going to fucking kill you," I growl, stalking toward him, but Ettie gets in my way, while at the same time, ripping the rubber band from her arm that Four used when drawing her blood.

"Just tell us, Seven."

"Sorry, Little One. It just tasted plain to me. Not even that extra tanginess I get with AB Negative."

"Thank God," she cries and then before I can push her away to kill Seven, she jumps in my arms.

"Leo! Do you know what this means?" she cries excitedly.

"It means exactly what I told you before," Four replies, sounding bored. "Blood bonds just are, they're gifts to our people. They don't make us act outside of our own free will. Sadly, this was anti-climatic."

"Maybe for you," I grumble, holding Ettie close. "If I ever have to watch another man drink Ettie's blood, I'll kill them."

"Understandable. It won't be an issue though if you complete the blood bond," Four says, yawning. "Let us go Stark, these two will be needing privacy."

"Complete the blood bond? What do you mean?" I ask, before I can stop myself. I don't want to ever live through this again. If I can put a stop to it, I'll do it immediately.

"Give her a drop of your blood. Just a drop or two every so often is all that is needed."

"What does that do?" Ettie asks, and from the look of distaste on her face I'm not sure she'll ever agree to it.

"It will slow your aging to be more in alignment with our kind, for one."

Ettie looks at me and blinks. Until this moment, we didn't understand that aging for either of us was different. There's so much I don't know. Maybe I need to start seeking Four out more to learn. It's clear he knows more than he's ever volunteered before.

"What else?" I ask, before he can leave.

"It will turn her blood into acid if any of our kind try and drink from her. It's a very handy little feature. I suggest you do it soon."

"Wait. Hold up for a minute. It will turn her blood to acid?"

"Don't worry, Stark," Four murmurs. "It won't affect the blood you've already digested."

"Well, I get that. But what would have happened if she'd already tasted Leo's blood before I drank any? I could have fucking died. Don't you think you should have warned me?"

"I know! That's why I said this was anti-climatic. Think of how exciting all of this would have been if that had happened. It would have been so much more fun. I do like surprises," Four says, just as the door closes.

Ettie begins to giggle and I look down into her eyes. She smiles up at me with such happiness, the anger inside of me leaves.

"Oracle is a little twisted," she murmurs.

"Don't you ever do this shit to me again. I don't think I could handle it," I warn.

"It won't be an issue any longer, because you're going to drink and stay healthy."

"Ettie—"

"And I'll do the same, so no one else can touch me but you."

With that one simple statement, she takes all the fight out of me. I groan as I take her in my arms and kiss her.

"I love you."

"I love you, too, Leo."

Maybe one of the best things about our connection—at least right now—is that we can tell each other how we feel and I don't have to stop kissing her.

37

Ettie

"What are you doing?" I murmur, as Leo begins undressing.

He carried us to our room and I didn't argue. I'm still nervous about how pale he's looking, but he carried me pretty easily. Still, I wish he would have taken at least a small drink. I can't lie. Some of this is so weird and strange to me, but Leo is my life. I don't want anything to happen to him.

"I'm going to take what you're offering me and then I'm going push you over the bed and spank your ass red."

"Uh…I don't think—"

"Don't worry, Sunshine. You'll like it and just to make sure, I'll fuck you so hard that you will be begging for more," he growls. I bite my lip as an all over body tremble moves through me and I feel the inside of my thighs go wet. Leo grins and I know he saw my reaction. I don't even care, because he's naked now, except for his jeans, and his fingers are already unzipping those. "No arguments?"

"I can't think of one," I respond without thinking, my mind focused on the way his cock springs out of his pants the minute the zipper is down. I never thought about sex much before, not until Leo came back into my life. Heck, I never thought about men in general. But, suddenly, I'm very glad that Leo goes commando so often.

"Good, now get undressed, Sunshine."

I look at him and he's smiling at me, but I see the need etched on his face, the spark of hunger in his eyes. I watch him as I undress. We don't talk, but somehow this seems like the most erotic thing we've shared together, me undressing while he stands before me naked, his cock hard, the head coated in his precum.

"Finished," I murmur, feeling as if my body is charged with electricity as I push my panties to the floor and step out of them.

"God, you're so damn gorgeous, Ettie," he groans, making me feel warm all over.

"So are you," I murmur bravely, closing the distance between us and taking his cock into my hand. He's so hot, firm yet flexible. I squeeze him and stroke him slowly, watching as that simple movement makes more precum leak from the head, a fine strand glazing my finger.

"You keep that up, Sunshine and my plans will derail, and I can't allow that to happen," Leo rumbles, his hand coming out to stop me from stroking him again.

"I'm just playing," I whine, taking my hand away. "I think you're beautiful, Leo. I want to learn everything about you." As I confess my thoughts to him, I bring my hand to my mouth and lick the back of my fingers that have his precum there. I hear Leo hiss in reaction, his body jerking, his hand going to my hip, as his fingers bite into my flesh.

"*Fuck*," he groans.

I moan as I taste him and I've barely swallowed the flavor down before Leo takes my mouth so rough and passionately that I lose my breath. His kiss is violent as he plunders my mouth like a warrior, claiming it and leaving me helpless to do anything but give him what he wants.

When we break apart, we're somehow at the bed and he

turns me so that my back is to him. This is all so new to me, but I've never been more excited than I am right now. He exerts pressure on the small of my back, urging me to bend forward. Desire and nerves have me trembling, but I do it without thought. Whatever happens next, I want. There's no denying that. It's not like my man is human, he's so much more than that. But, I suddenly feel sorry for the millions of girls out there that can't have their own Leo. They can't have mine, though. I'm never letting him go.

He belongs to me. I gasp as his hand moves to the crevice of my ass, his fingers creating magic in their wake.

"We belong to each other." Leo corrects me, letting me know he hears my thoughts, so I take a moment to let down any shields I might have inadvertently put up. I want him to feel my love, my pleasure and…*my joy.*

"My sweet, sweet, Ettie," Leo groans from behind me. Like this, I can't see what he's doing, but I feel the moment his cock slides between my legs. His hand is wrapped around the shaft and he purposely rakes it against my pussy, coating it in my desire.

"Leo, hurry," I moan, because it feels like forever since I've made love with him—even if it hasn't been.

"Do you need me, Sunshine?" he asks, the head of his cock pushing inside of me just a little. Immediately, my inner muscles try to latch onto him, needing him deeper inside. My knees quiver as my fingers bite into the sheets of our bed.

"Always," I groan.

"Do you need my cock inside of you?" he purrs, his hot breath branding my skin as he kisses the side of my neck. I can't respond with much more than a throaty moan as I feel his lips, and his teeth rake against my neck, not pricking the skin but I instinctively know that's coming soon. "I'm going to thrust inside of you like this, Ettie, fuck you so hard that you will feel me every time you take a step and ache to have me back." I can't even be embarrassed at the flood of desire that escapes, drenching his cock. I'm so ready to come that one thrust and I'll go over the edge, I know it. I rock back into him, the sheets sliding against my nipples feeling like a caress.

"Leo," I beg, my body feeling like a live wire with sparks shooting all around me.

"You could come just like this, couldn't you my little, Ettie? I wouldn't even have to fuck you and you'd still shatter for me, wouldn't you?" I don't respond, there's no point. We both know the truth and his dirty questions are just making me more turned on, hotter, wetter and ready to explode. His hand wraps in my hair, pulling the tendrils tight and sending a quick burst of pain as he thrusts deep inside of me.

"Leo," I cry out, feeling him bottom out against me, his cock so deep inside it's almost painful. He doesn't move. I squeeze against his cock, needing more, but he refuses to give it.

"You're mine, Ettie. I get what you were doing, but you don't give any part of yourself to anyone but me ever again," he growls, his voice a vibrating rumble that causes my pussy to clench, tightening everything in me. When I don't respond his hand comes down on my ass, spanking it hard, fire and pain radiating and combining to make this explosion of pleasure inside of me, so intense that I can do little more than whine. "Promise me," he growls.

"I promise," I gasp.

With the words that he wants from me, he begins fucking me, withdrawing just to thrust back in. He fucks me hard, and I lunge back to meet his strokes, loving it and wanting more. His fingers bite into my hips with bruising force as he takes control. Moving my body how he wants me, fucking me so hard that I could see stars and giving me more pleasure than I've ever experienced before.

"Who do you belong to, Ettie?"

"You, Leo. I belong to you."

"That's my girl," he groans and I can feel his cock jerk inside of me and warmth coat my insides. "Mine," he gasps.

I know he's coming and I'm so close, but there's one more thing I need.

"Leo, bite me…take my blood," I growl, suddenly knowing that the bond is natural, that I want his bite, that I *need* it.

I don't have to ask him twice. He kisses the side of my neck and then a second later I feel a slight sting and then so much pleasure I almost lose consciousness. He moans against my skin as he tastes me and I explode into a million pieces, climaxing now that I know I belong to Leo in every way possible.

38

Leo

"Tell me about your scars, Sunshine," I murmur, kissing the side of her neck as my fingers drift over her back. She's lying on her stomach in our bed, her head tilted to the side to look at me, her brown eyes are shining, her lips swollen from our love making and are stretched in a satisfied smile. She's so beautiful it hurts.

I didn't give her my blood and she didn't ask. I don't know why, other than the moment was so perfect that I didn't want to force something on her that she might not be ready for. I know it will happen and soon. For now, knowing that we're bonded, that she belongs to me, is enough.

"Do they...disgust you, Leo?" she asks, her voice quiet and for a moment I see shame cloud her beautiful face.

"There's nothing about you that could disgust me, Ettie... Not a damn thing. I just want to know."

"Why? It can't change anything. It's in the past."

"Humor me, Baby," I beg, and I can't explain it to her, but I just need to know. When she got these, I wasn't there to protect her. I should have been. Five years I've been free and I left her back there for way too long, because...

Fuck, there's no other way to say it. I just wanted my freedom. I didn't want to go back to check on Ettie, because that would have meant I might get captured again. All I could think about was finally, after being tortured and a prisoner for my whole life, I was free. Freedom is all I ever wanted. I didn't realize what Ettie meant to me. I had no idea that she would be my purpose for living…that she would be my salvation. She fills the emptiness inside of me that nothing else ever could.

"When you escaped, my mother blamed me. Her punishment was more severe than normal," she says simply. Her and I both know it's much worse than she's telling me. I close my eyes as a wave of pain threatens to drown me.

"Stop, Leo. It's not your fault."

"You sought me out after my escape. I remember hearing the fear in your voice."

"It's not important. It's in the past now."

"I'm sorry, Sunshine. I'm so fucking sorry. I—"

"Stop, Leo," she whispers, reaching up to put her fingers on my lips. "You just got your freedom, it was too dangerous for you to come back to me. I may not have understood when I was younger, but I do now."

I take her hand, pulling her fingers away from my lips and placing a kiss against her palm, before bringing her hand back against my heart.

"That's not it, Ettie. I promise you, if I had been able, I would have come back to you. I'd been shot, we'd spent so much time putting distance between us and Draven's compound that I was really weak. Even hearing your voice, I couldn't help. Then, after I healed a little, you were just gone. I tried to contact you, even when I could feel nothing but the emptiness, I kept trying."

"It's okay. We have each other now, Leo."

"That we do and I'm never letting you go."

"I'm not going anywhere. There's not been one day that I haven't missed you. I might have just been a little girl, but even then I knew that you were all I ever wanted. I loved you then, and I love you now, it's just a little different kind of love," she adds with a smile, which leads me to pulling her mouth to mine and taking it in a kiss that hopefully shows her just how much I care about her.

"It's starting to feel like I'm dreaming, Leo," she whispers, her voice almost a hum, sleepy and filled with pleasure.

"No way," I tell her with a grin. "Dreams can never be this good. I know because I've been having dreams about you. This is much better."

"You've been dreaming about me?" she asks, her smile deepening.

"Oh yeah," I groan as I roll over on my back and take her with me. She's lying over me, my fingers instantly tangling into her hair. "Definitely." I push against her body, letting her feel my hard cock thrusting against her wet depths, needing her again.

"Were these dreams G-rated?" She giggles as she asks, rubbing against me. She's wet and warm and I just want to bury myself inside of her.

"Never," I laugh, not even bothering to lie. The word comes out as a tortured moan, as her hand moves down to wrap around my cock.

"God, Sunshine." She strokes my cock, her hand holding me tightly, our gazes locked on one another and I commit the moment to my memory, because I know in my heart there's nothing better than this look on her face and the pleasure in my body. "I love you."

"Love you," she purrs, her body shifting against mine, her words breathless. She wants more and God knows I definitely need more.

"I want you again, Sunshine."

"Please," she gasps, as she positions my cock at her opening. It's all I can do to keep from thrusting inside. I don't want to hurt her, I push her hair from her face, my hand pressing against her neck as I tilt her face exactly where I want it.

"You're not too sore?" I ask, worried about her because she

was so tight earlier and I know I'm not small. The last thing I want to do is hurt her.

"Never. Make me yours again, Leo," she begs.

"You are mine, Ettie. You will always be mine," I promise, as I slide inside of her. My eyes close as the pleasure pushes through me. When I open them again, it's to look directly into Ettie's beautiful brown beauties and the love and peace I see in them is everything.

She's everything.

39

Leo

One Month Later

THERE'S an old saying that all good things must come to an end. I've never thought much about it. Life is life and you just have to live it, but things always change, so I figured the saying was true. The last month with Ettie has been what I imagine living in paradise would be like. Every day just keeps getting better. Even with dissension within our numbers, it's still been the happiest days of my life.

Honestly, without Ettie, I'm not sure I'd still be here. I might actually hit the road. Our members are fighting and there's a clear division line. Six and Eight are not happy here. They've always been different from the rest of us, but those differences are becoming more and more evident. They are bitching about everything, most notably the fact that we need blood to survive. It disgusts them. You would think the fact that they were made and raised in the same lab that we were would make them more understanding—but, that's clearly not the thing. They despise Scar—and that's one name Ettie has given that I can easily recall. It fits Five to a tee. None of us truly seem to click with Scar, but he's one of us. Ettie is uneasy around him, and she's warned me not to trust him. When I question her about it, however, all she can say is it's a feeling that she has. Six and Scar were in a huge fight yesterday, it took four of us to pull them off of each other. The strangest thing happened. Eight changed into a wolf and attacked Scar, going for his jugular. I suppose that's his power, but shapeshifting is new to all of us and when Seven asked to do some tests on them, they refused. We've all agreed that the more tests we do, the more we'll understand who we are and what is vital to our survival. The fact that they are refusing, along with their disgust with the need for blood we have, is making a clear division line and only seems to be growing as time passes.

I'm sitting in the common area now, which consists of a bunch of couches, a pool table, a couple of old arcade games that Seven found somewhere and refurbished, and a kitchen with a bar. I'm sipping on a beer and evidence of the division is here, because Six and Eight are all the way on the other side of the room from me and a couple of the others. The only time they interact with us at all anymore is when Ettie is around. They like her and are respectful with her. At least I'm grateful for that. I couldn't handle it if they hurt her feelings. I'd have to react then—I won't let anyone disrespect Ettie. Just the thought of it makes me angry.

"Leo! Quick come to the lab!" Seven yells from the door. He doesn't come in, instead he runs down the opposite way. Immediately, fear fills me. On instinct, my mind searches out Ettie. I know for a fact she is in the lab with Oracle. She always meets with him for a couple hours every day. They seem to really like each other and somehow her presence is making our leader stable.

"Ettie, Sunshine, are you okay?"

"Pain..." she cries inside of my brain and for a minute I can

feel excruciating pain and then it's like a wall slams down severing our connection.

I take off running, going so fast that my surroundings blur. I even pass Seven, and I'm inside the lab before he even gets there. Ettie is lying on an exam table, she's curled into the fetal position, both of her hands covering her head as she pulls it down and she's moaning in pain. I go straight to her, picking her up in my arms, pushing Oracle out of my way. Ettie's body is shaking, as she moans in pain.

"What's going on?" I demand, my voice a quiet rumble. "What did you do to her?"

"It's nothing I've done, Leo. This is coming from an outside source. She's got loud screeching noises, high frequency tones bombarding her."

"What the fuck does that mean?"

"I'm not sure I know," Oracle mutters. He has his back turned to me and when he turns around, he's holding a huge needle.

"What are you going to do with that?" I'm literally yelling at him. Every protective urge in my body coming out. I don't want anyone touching her.

"Hopefully knock her out, until we can put up some kind of defense bubble around her."

"Coming... For..." Ettie mumbles, her eyes closed, her head rocking up and down as she tries to talk to me.

"Coming for? Shhh...Ettie...don't try to talk. We're going to fix this. I promise, we'll fix this," I promise her and I have no idea what I'm telling her. I don't know what's going on, so it's hard to fix, but I'll find a way. *I have to.*

"Can you hear what's going on in her head?" Oracle asks. I frown trying to push in... "I can feel our connection but there's like a steel fence pushed around it that I can't seem to break through," I explain. I try again, but it's useless.

"She's blocking you, possibly trying to protect you."

"Why would she do that?"

"I don't know, Leo, maybe it's painful and she's trying to spare you? Maybe she doesn't even realize she's doing it."

"She's protecting me," I mutter at once.

"That would be my guess," Oracle confirms.

Seven is standing beside me now, I can feel him there, even if I don't look up.

"We have to do something," I tell him, as Ettie's whimpering begins to get louder. Whatever is happening is torturing her.

"We are," Oracle says and before I can question him again or stop him, he plunges a needle into Ettie's arm.

"Damn it—" I hiss, anger vibrating in me, my fangs elongating and this time something new happens to me. My damn fingernails try to extend out to fine points, almost claws—but not quite that big and lethal.

"Calm down, Young One. It's just a sedative. If she's knocked out, they can't get to her."

"No one touches her or does anything to her without my permission," I order, not giving a fuck who I am talking to. I reach out into Ettie's mind again. "Damn it, Ettie, stop blocking me."

"This wouldn't be an issue if you had completed the blood bond," Oracle chastises.

I ignore him and just as Ettie goes limp in my arms, her shield breaks down enough that I can hear the high-pitched screaming over and over, all repeating one thing.

"I'm coming for you."

```
┌─────────────────────────────────────┐
│                                       │
│                 40                    │
│                                       │
│                Ettie                  │
│                                       │
└─────────────────────────────────────┘
```

"Leo," I moan, feeling as if I've been kicked repeatedly in the head over and over—by a steel-toed boot. At least the screaming has stopped. I thought I was going to die.

"I'm here, Ettie. I'm right here," Leo answers immediately, and I feel my hand wrapped in his, his breath against the side of my face. "Are you okay?"

I look around and immediately realize I'm in the lab still, but that now the lights are dimmed. I'm also not on the table anymore. Instead, I'm in Leo's arms and he's sitting in an over-sized chair that I've never seen in here before. That means I must have been out for quite a while now.

"Ettie?" Leo prompts and I struggle to try and focus.

"I'm okay," I murmur, feeling anything but.

"Who was that in your head?" Leo asks.

"You heard?" I gasp, shocked, because I did my best not to let him know.

"I did and you trying to block me out of that beautiful, but stubborn, little head of yours better not happen again."

"Leo, I didn't—"

"We're a team, Ettie. No secrets. Got it?"

"I was trying to protect you," I grumble, refusing to feel guilty for wanting to spare Leo from my pain.

"No secrets ever, even if it is just you trying to protect me. Actually, scratch that. No secrets from me ever, *especially* if it's you trying to protect me," he demands.

"You mean that if the roles were reversed, you wouldn't try and protect me, Leo?" I know the answer before he even gives it, but still I press it, hoping he will see how crazy he's being.

"That's different," he says, shaking his head.

"Bullshit."

"Quit distracting me, Ettie. Do you want to tell me how Draven is talking in your head?"

I blink, unable to talk and not quite sure if I'm breathing. It has been so long since I've even heard Draven's voice that I honestly didn't realize it was him until this moment. I shudder as the implications of that hit me.

It was Draven telling me that he was coming for me.

"I don't know," I mumble. "I didn't even realize until just now that it was him, Leo. I'm nothing to him, I've barely even seen him, unless Mom took me to work and he was there. I could see my mother coming for me, but why would he?" I ask him questions that I know he can't answer, I can taste the panic on my tongue. My mother is cruel, but if Draven is hunting for me...*He's pure evil.* Chills run through me and if Leo wasn't holding me right now, I would probably take off running.

"He's never spoken to you in your head like that before?" Stark asks, and I shake my head no.

"Never," I deny. "And, this was different from our connection, Leo. This was painful and there was this high-pitched squealing that hurt to hear."

"Is that it?" Oracle asks.

"There were screams and they just kept filling my head as he talked. He was repeating the same thing over and over and the longer it went on, the louder and more painful it all became."

"How long did it last, Sunshine?"

I look up at Leo and shrug, because I have no idea. He holds me closer, kissing the top of my head.

"Luciana says ten minutes, give or take a second or two," Oracle responds. "It is all quiet now, yes?"

"Yes," I respond with a nod. "There's nothing but a dull throbbing pain and a ringing in my ears."

"Some of that could be the drugs used to knock you out. I doubled the normal dose. Sorry about that, fledgling."

I blink at the nickname; not sure I like it. I don't argue however. I know it wouldn't do any good.

"We need to figure out how to stop this from happening again," Leo demands.

"That answer is most simple," Oracle says. "The larger question is the one you should be asking, Leo."

"What's that?" we both ask simultaneously.

"How do we keep Draven away from her?" he asks and I can't stop the shiver that moves over me. Leo holds me tighter and I close my eyes trying to soak in his warmth. The truth is, I'm terrified. All this time, I've been worried about my mother finding me. I never thought about Draven being the one that was coming after me. If he gets me...

I won't survive.

41

Leo

Five Weeks Later

"I DON'T LIKE THIS, damn it."

"Leo, I have to get out, I was going insane. I was a prisoner at my mother's, the last thing I want to do is be a prisoner here in Montana, too."

"It's different, Ettie," I growl, frustrated because no one is listening to me.

"You should know better than that, Leo. A prison is still a prison, if you don't have any freedom. I refuse to hide and cower. If I do that, then Draven wins regardless."

"It won't be forever, Ettie, but we need to be careful until we locate him," I explain for what feels like the hundredth time. Ettie seems to ignore me for the hundredth and one times.

"We've been trying to find him for over a month now and we can't. All we truly know is that his compound is empty and that's only because of Four's contacts. Draven not being there, could mean anything."

"It means he's moved and he's closer to us, I know it."

"Leo, you don't have any proof of that."

"I don't need proof, I can feel it."

"He's probably right," Seven says, weighing in.

"And maybe he's not," Six adds and I throw him a look designed to make his balls freeze and fall off. He laughs. Bastard hasn't found his Ettie yet. If he had, he'd know how important those balls of his are.

We're at a bar on the outskirts of Billings. It's about an hour away from our compound, so that we can lose anyone that might follow us back, but close enough we can get back in a hurry if needed. Music is slamming through the place, and alcohol is flowing freely. We're here to celebrate Eight's birthday, although I think everyone planned it to get Ettie out and to stop obsessing over Draven. We're all looking over our shoulders so much that we are jumpy as fucking hell.

I pull Ettie closer to my body, my arm wrapping around her front. She tilts her neck for me, exposing the area I dream of biting—but have resisted so far. I kiss it now, instead, but I hum as I feel her pulse quicken.

"Come home with me, Ettie. I'll make you feel so good you'll think you're flying, you will feel so free."

"Let's just enjoy tonight, please Leo? Tomorrow, I promise I'll go back into hiding and let you guys take over trying to locate Draven, who, by the way, could be anywhere," she responds.

"Yeah," I murmur, thinking he could be here and that is what scares me.

"Okay, Ettie, the guys and I have been talking and they want to know when it's our turn," Eight pipes up.

"Your turn?" Ettie asks, and I shake my head at Eight, because I know what they're talking about. I'm dreading it—mostly because if Ettie does what they ask, I'll have to change what I call everyone. They all want names like me, apparently like Seven—who everyone but me seems to call Stark easily, and

Four—who even I call Oracle when I'm around him, because he refuses to answer to anything else.

"We all want names," Ten responds. Of all of us, he is the quietest. He keeps himself distant from everyone else. He seems like a decent guy, but I can't seem to get a handle on him.

Ettie laughs and I swear I will never get used to how happy that sound makes me.

"Can't you pick your own names? Stark did," she points out.

"Yeah, but his name is lame."

"Fuck you, Six. My name is A-mazing."

"Whatever. So, Ettie? Will you do it?"

She looks around at all of the guys, and smiles. She's happy. She likes them, and for the most part they're my family—at least the only one I've ever had, so that's a good thing. All of them are here, with the exception of Five—Scar. He didn't want to join and the fact that he isn't here made Ettie relax more. She really doesn't like him and to be honest, I'm not sure I like him myself, so I can understand.

"I can, I suppose," she says, sounding excited. "If you're sure this is what you want."

"Definitely," Eight responds, nodding his head.

"I hope one of you motherfuckers likes the name Mufasa," Seven snarls. "There's not a damn thing wrong with Stark. It's a lot better than Leo."

"I'm pretty partial to the name Leo. Especially when Ettie is moaning it in my ear," I tell him and the bastard flips me off.

"That's cold man. I'm going to go get a drink, maybe I'll find my Ettie at the bar," he grumbles, stomping off.

"I can't believe you said that, Leo," Ettie whispers, her cheeks blushed a deep red.

"I love the way you are with me, Ettie. Sometimes a man who has everything feels the need to brag."

"Whatever," she grouses, rolling her eyes.

"Eight, you're Jacob."

"Jacob? That seems kind of lame next to the name Scar or Oracle. It is better than Leo, I suppose." I flip him off.

"Trust me. Jacob is perfect. There was this movie and the guy had the earthy, sexy vibe going, like you do, and he was a total babe. He also had a…shall we say a love of wolves, like you do?"

"What is this movie?" Eight asks, but I don't let Ettie answer.

"Sexy? You're not allowed to notice any man is sexy except me, Ettie."

"Say what?"

"You heard me. I'm the only man you can ever find sexy."

"You're a little insane, Leo. I didn't say I thought of Eight as anything other than a friend. He is hot, though."

"Thanks, Ettie," Eight laughs.

"You better mean hot as in he's melting because it's two hundred degrees," I warn her.

She doesn't respond to that, she just kisses my lips. It's not much, but it at least shows the bastards at the table that she belongs to me, so I let it drop—for now.

"What about me?" Six asks.

"Axel."

"Axel? Damn I like that. That's the best name yet," Six grins, like he won some damn prize.

"What made you think of that name?" I ask, curious.

"I just always liked the name. I imagined one day, if I ever had a child, I'd name him Axel. I don't think that's going to happen now, so…" she shrugs. I frown. Does she think we won't have kids? Fuck. Can we have them? Have her and Oracle discussed it and she believes it's impossible? I'm going to have to get to the bottom of this. I want Ettie to have everything she's ever wanted and if that's kids and if I can't father children, then we will find a way for her to have them.

"Pick another name. He can't have that one."

"Damn it, Leo. I like that name."

"I'll cry you a river later. Ettie and I are keeping that name. Think of another for him, Sunshine."

She looks at me and even without our connection, I can feel the happiness and pleasure she's feeling. I kiss her forehead, closing my eyes at the wave of love I feel moving between us.

"It better be cool, or I'm using Axel anyway," Six warns.

"Endy," Ettie says and everyone frowns.

"Indie? As in Indiana Jones?" Seven asks, joining us again.

"You watch too much television," I mutter.

"No, this is after Endymion. He was supposed to be a Greek mortal who was a shepherd in the fields."

"Well, that sounds boring as hell," Six mutters.

"The goddess of the moon, Selene, fell in love with him and bore him like fifty daughters."

"Shit, fifty? Is that even possible?" Eight asks.

"She was a goddess," Ettie says, like that explains it all and maybe it does.

"Moon goddess? I can dig it. Endy it is," Six responds, sounding really satisfied.

"That leaves me. What's my name going to be, Ettie?" Ten asks.

Ettie looks him over carefully. "Sean," she whispers.

"Sean?"

"Another movie character. This one was my favorite love story. Sean was a retired boxer who accidentally killed someone in the ring. He moved to Ireland to discover his heritage and forget what happened and a fiery red-head helps heal him. They love almost as much as they fight."

"You're a hopeless romantic, Ettie," Ten murmurs.

"I guess so. I can name you something else," she murmurs, sounding self-conscious.

"I like Sean. Who knows? Maybe I'll find my...what was the girl's name?"

"Mary Kate," Ettie responds.

"Maybe I'll find my Mary Kate," he says.

"Fuck. Do you feel that?" Six—Endy—growls. All of us look at each other, because we all feel it. A heaviness comes over us. The kind of sensation we only get when there is about to be trouble. If the intensity of this feeling is anything to go by, it's going to be really bad.

I immediately grab Ettie's hand and rise.

"Let's get the fuck out of here," I growl. Six and Seven take the lead and the others surround Ettie, protecting her. We move as a unit, but the feeling just keeps intensifying. Whatever is behind it, isn't good. If it's Draven, then this isn't going to end well. I need to make sure I get Ettie to safety.

I can't let anything happen to her.

42

Ettie

"Maybe it's nothing," I whisper, hoping I'm right as Leo holds me to him and leads me toward the back door of the club.

"Maybe," Leo whispers back, but the tightness in his voice makes it clear he doesn't believe that.

"I'm sorry, Leo. I should have listened to you."

"Shh… Ettie. We'll get home. Everything will be okay."

Guilt swamps me. I should have listened, but I really was going stir crazy. Leo might not have said anything, but I knew him and the others were dying to get out. Most of them—with the exception of Scar and Oracle, have spent most of their life in captivity. I didn't want to be the reason that they spent more of it like that.

We make it to the door without incident and I'm starting to feel safer. The same can't be said of the men surrounding me. If anything, they look ready to fight a war. I try to look around them, but I can only see small flashes because of everyone's hulking shoulders and bodies. I really should have been taller if I was going to live around giants.

"Finally."

I run into Stark's back as everyone comes to a stop. Leo

174

moves me behind his back. I try to stop the trembling that tries to hit my body, because I know that voice.

Draven.

"Leo..."

"Shh... he might be able to hear us, Ettie. It will be okay."

"No, Eleven, it's not going to be okay. Where is little Esther? I always hated that name. Your mother insisted on it and because I wasn't ready to kill her, I let her have her way. Show yourself, Esther," he commands.

His voice alone sends chills down my spine. Fear swamps me and causes a fine bead of sweat to break out all over my body.

"She's not getting near you," Leo growls, his voice deadly. *"Stay put,"* he tells me, through our connection. I can't respond. It feels like Draven is in my head again, the loud screeching noises aren't there, but I can feel his presence and it's stronger than it was before. It's almost overpowering and he's telling me to walk to him—only without words. It's taking everything I have not to do it. My feet shuffle in the gravel beneath my shoes as I try to resist. I tightly squeeze my eyes shut, my body shaking as I try to resist him.

"Eleven. You held such promise, but you never developed. It's sad really. You're nothing but a waste of space, except for one small thing, you're weak."

"Let Ettie and the others out of here and I'll show you exactly how strong I am, Draven."

"Leo, no," I cry. I move toward him, giving up fighting Draven's command when Stark grabs my arm, refusing to let me leave. "Let me go. I have to help him. Draven will kill him!" I hiss.

Stark just shakes his head no. I pull and tug, but it doesn't do any good.

"Leo, no," Draven repeats, badly imitating my voice—his full of disgust. "It's humiliating that my Esther has taken up with the likes of you, Eleven. Still, I suppose it's better than getting fleas with the dogs."

Endy and Jacob jerk at Draven's slur. The emotions swirling from each of them are so intense they threaten to drown me. There's so much anger that it's suffocating me. The only thing that is keeping me focused is the surety in Draven's mind that he's going to kill Leo.

"Quit stalling, Draven. Let them go, and you and I can finally deal with this shit."

"Now, you're just amusing me, Eleven. Do you really think you can handle me?"

"I know I can," Leo says and I want to believe the confidence in his voice, but I don't. Draven's going to kill him.

I have to do something.

"I'm defending my mate. I know I can," Leo responds, his voice deadly.

"Mate? My, my, you've been busy. I thought that might be the case when LaDawna told me that Esther was the one that helped you escape. But, I began to discredit her report when it became clear you hadn't blood bonded with one another."

I look through the legs of the others and I can see Leo advancing toward Draven. I whimper, unable to keep the sound to myself.

"That's where you're wrong. I guess you don't know everything, do you, Draven?" Leo taunts. Everyone around me grows still as Draven advances. I've maneuvered enough that I can see Draven now and I can't help but notice that he seems to float as he walks, much like Oracle does.

"Oh, I smell her on you. You've sipped from my Esther, didn't you? How did she taste? Delicious, I bet."

"She's not yours. She will never be yours. I don't know how you got in her head, but that won't happen again. Ettie belongs to me."

"You're so foolish. I think it's time to give you a little lesson in our power, fledgling."

I blink when I hear Draven call Leo that. That's the same thing Oracle called me.

Is it just a coincidence?

"You can try, but you need to let the others go. We both know your fight is with me. I'm the one who escaped and took the others with me."

"Maybe, but then, maybe not. Now, I can have you and all of my pretties back. So, I think I'll hold onto them."

"I never took you as a fool, Draven. Do you really think it's smart to try and take on all of us at once? That's one against five. You won't stand a chance."

"You'd think that, because you're stupid. You don't even try to learn and if I remember Four correctly, he does love teaching. It's a pity you refuse to listen. But don't worry, Eleven. I've decided I'm going to teach you and *now* is the time for your first lesson."

"I can hardly wait," Leo replies drolly.

"Such bravado. You're going to be a joy to train, Eleven," Draven laughs, but the sound doesn't sound comical or joyful at all. It's maniacal and cold as steel.

"Your first lesson is that you're a vampire. Vampires are not the myths humans make up because they can't deal with the fact that monsters lurk in the shadows. We're real and we've been around for centuries."

"When do we skip ahead to hear about Santa Claus?" Leo asks. "I'm a lab rat that you created, Draven, nothing more and nothing less. But, I'll also be the bastard to send you back to hell where you belong. That's where *mere* humans go, right? You really shouldn't have messed around making something that is stronger than you in every way."

"Eleven, don't try to bluff. You know what I am. We both do. What's more, I'm older than any you have encountered."

"You're boring me, Draven."

"Then, I suppose, I should get on with my lesson. You see, a vampire knows what no one else has managed to grasp."

"What's that?"

"We can control the world with our blood."

"Is that right?"

"Watch," Draven says. "Move away from Esther," he commands, his voice booming. I can feel the power in it, it's almost physical. Then, one by one, all of the men surrounding me step away.

"What are you doing?" Leo growls. "Protect her!" I see the anguish in Seven's face. I know he's trying, but he can't overcome Draven's command. Leo moves back to stand in front of me, but for the first time, I can feel his panic.

"It's been years since you've been fed my blood and yet, every one of you are still under my command. You see, Eleven? There's power in our blood. We can make the strongest of creatures crawl, even the little doggies. Roll over on your stomach, Six," he demands, and I see claws begin to sap through and Six's bones try to shift. He's fighting the command with everything in him. "But, don't shift." Just like that—mid-shift even—Six is frozen, dropping to the ground and lying there on his stomach. It makes Draven laugh and this time there is pleasure in it.

"You bastard," Eight yells, but it does nothing but make Draven laugh some more. "On your knees, dog," he growls and Eight drops even quicker than Six, helpless to do anything but remain on his knees staring at Draven. Draven glides to him and then delivers a kick to Eight's gut that sends him back a good ten feet. The others do nothing, but I think they're trying, they just *can't.* I run to Eight, narrowly escaping Leo's hand that reaches behind him to try and stop me.

"You see, Leo? I can control everyone. Except you, but then, you've replaced my blood bond with that of Esther's, haven't you?"

"Ettie, get back here now," Leo yells, and he doesn't hide the panic in his voice.

"But, Eight—"

"Now, Ettie!" he growls and I start to pull away from Eight. Then, I stop. My gaze locks with Draven's.

"Come to me, Esther." I want to deny him, I try with everything in me, but the order in his voice right now is even stronger than it was in my head before. My feet begin walking toward Draven, and I can't look away from him...

No matter how hard I try.

"Ettie! Stop! What are you doing?"

"Haven't you figured it out, yet, Leo?"

"Leave her alone, you bastard."

"Esther is as much under my control as the others, probably more so."

"You fed her your blood? You monster. She was only a little girl."

"I didn't have to feed her my blood, Leo. She was born with it running through her veins," Draven murmurs so softly that I'm amazed I can hear him. *But, I do.* I hear his words and bile rises inside of me. I see the truth in his eyes, even before he responds to Leo. "Esther is my daughter, Eleven."

My knees threaten to buckle at his announcement, but I don't let them. I just stand there looking at the face of a monster.

The face of my...father.

```
┌─────────────────────────────────────┐
│                                      │
│                 43                   │
│                                      │
│                Leo                   │
│                                      │
└─────────────────────────────────────┘
```

H is daughter.

Fuck, how did I miss that? Normal humans don't have the abilities that Ettie have, right? It should have been a clue from day one. Fuck. What does this even mean?

"I didn't know Leo. I swear, I didn't know."

"We'll talk about it later, Ettie. Fight his control. You can do it."

I do my best to keep any of my emotions out of my head. I don't want Ettie feeling worse. It's not her fault that Draven is her father. Right now, I have to stay focused.

"Such a good girl, now sit there and behave while I kill the little vampire who thought he could claim you," Draven says, his pale, gnarled hand reaching out to pat Ettie on the top of her head.

He really is an ugly motherfucker. He's pale, as if he never sees the sun outside and I have a feeling he hasn't. His hair is jet black and so long that I'm sure he'd sit on it if he didn't keep it braided and folded in half, the bottom secured to the top of his head. His hands are misshapen, like someone with severe arthritis because they're bent and drawn in unnatural directions. He's wearing deep jet-black pants and a shirt. If his face wasn't so pale, he'd blend into the night. He looks nothing like Ettie, with maybe the exception of her hair color.

"I hate to cut our reunion short, Eleven, but I need to get rid of you. With the connection you've forged with my Esther, I can't be sure you won't try to use her to escape again."

"What could you possibly want with Ettie? You barely looked at her for years."

"That's because I thought she was hopelessly human like her mother. Our kind need a mate to breed. Imagine my surprise when mine was a mere human. It was disappointing, but I admit I had hope our offspring would be strong. Imagine my surprise when not only was it a girl, but one that was proving to be nothing more than a mere mortal."

"It must have been humbling to realize that a mere human's DNA was stronger than yours," I prod him, rewarded with a spark of anger on his face. I can definitely see how that has hurt his ego over the years.

"That's what that bitch led me to believe. We both know that's not true though, don't we? I killed her for her insolence."

Ettie gasps, but I can't look at her. I know she hated her mother, but it has to be hard to hear of her murder in such an off-hand way.

"You killed your mate? What about her blood?" I ask, curious, because I know I couldn't survive without Ettie's blood, it's one of the reasons I hated to drink from her—afraid she'd think I only loved her because she keeps me alive.

"The bond you mean? You really do know nothing. Four is slipping, but then he's always been more insane than sane, ever since Luciana succumbed."

"Succumbed?"

"I didn't need LaDawna's blood to survive after her death. Nothing severs a blood bond like death, Eleven. I probably won't have another mate out there. Our kind seems to only get one of those. Still, we survive just fine once the bond has been severed. I told you, our blood is our strength and it always wants us to survive, Eleven. I had hopes though that once you bonded with Esther, that you would be under my control. Apparently, it works differently when it's not direct blood. That's disappointing, but good knowledge to have nevertheless. Knowledge is power, Eleven. Perhaps if you all had sought it, you wouldn't be at my mercy now."

"If Esther is your child, who do we belong to?" I ask, unable to pass up the opportunity to find out how we were created. Draven is an asshole, but he's not wrong about knowledge. Right now, I'm wishing I had paid more attention to Four's ramblings.

"Now, that is the million-dollar question, Eleven. None of you are mine. LaDawna was never able to give me a son. She was weak and the one child she gave me was Esther. I had to get inventive. Tracking down halflings of our kind that had found their mate started as a past time. Then, I discovered one pregnant. It began as an experiment to feed her my blood to nourish the baby and then Six was born. I hoped the failure was because he was a dog. Still, it happened again with Eight, so it can't be a fluke. Luckily after Six, I already had Seven's mother in my possession, she could be bred by our kind and her mate didn't care, as long as he could fuck her when he wanted and had money in his pocket."

"So, you're saying he was a worthless piece of shit."

"That's a horrible way to talk about an old friend, Leo," Five says coming out from the darkness behind Draven. He walks to stand beside Draven, holding a gun and pointing it at me.

Shock hammers through me. I knew that Five was an asshole and we were all cautious around him, but to discover that he has betrayed us like this...

"I should be more surprised than I am," I growl.

"You were always kind of smart to be such an idiot about other things," Five shrugs.

"I'm afraid it's time to call an end to the fun. We need to get the others loaded into the containment vehicle and get out of here. I'm afraid you'll have to die Eleven. I have plans for Ettie and that can only happen when you're dead and the bond is clearly over."

"Plans for her?" I ask, knowing that whatever it is, won't be good, but unable to stop myself from asking.

"You are an inquisitive one. Sadly, Five's mate didn't survive the birth of Twelve. So, I need a new…incubator, if you will. Ettie will serve just fine."

I have to block out Ettie's cry of pain in my brain. I can't look at her right now, even as her fear floods through my mind. I have to stay focused. I have no idea how I'm going to get out of here, but I have to try. I have to try and get Ettie safe.

"You're forgetting one thing, Draven. I'm Ettie's mate, without me—"

"Oh, shoot. I forgot the most important part of your lesson, Eleven. Once your mate is dead and the bond is severed? You can fuck whoever you want, whenever you want," he laughs. "Five here has been dying to have a go at my daughter. Who knows? Maybe I will too."

"You touch her and I'll find a way to kill you, bring you back and kill you again," I warn him.

"Yes, I think I will," he continues, as if I didn't say a thing. "After all, what could be better than my own blood bearing my child."

"I'd kill myself first," Ettie hisses.

"You can't even stand unless I tell you, Esther," Draven laughs at her. "Now, are we finished with this lesson, Eleven? Or, do I need to go over how a naturally born vampire matures quickly? Did you know that you were all even rushed through that process? Once you were created, I fed chemicals into you and the surrogate to have you age quickly. Hell, before the whore died, she could get pregnant within a day and give birth within a month. Twelve reached adulthood in only one year. I'm sure Esther will do even better."

"You're sick," Ettie moans, fighting to stand and back away from her father. I can see her act of independence shocks Draven. Perhaps he doesn't know everything yet.

"What are you going to do, Esther? You have to know you can't stop this. Look at your friends over there. At my command, they're going to kill your mate. Then, with Eleven's blood still on their hands, they'll carry you to my car and walk into their own imprisonment. It's over, Esther. Don't be stupid like your mother and try to disobey me."

Esther begins walking toward them. At first, I'm certain he's making her. I go to join her when her voice booms clearly in my head, so loud and strong that it takes my breath. She's magnificent.

"No, Leo. I'm in control. I can end this. Trust me."

I still walk behind her. There's no way she's facing any of this alone. If I am to die here, I'll do it making sure Ettie is safe.

"What are you doing, daughter?"

"Don't call me that," Ettie says. "I'm not that, I'll never be that."

"Of course you are. Look how strong you are, even now. Trying to defy me. It's so cute."

"I'm going to kill you," Ettie says simply, and shock and fuck, even admiration flares all over Draven's face.

"You are my child," he says, with so much pleasure it's sickening. "I'll enjoy that later. For now, I must kill all of your friends. Attack each other until death," he orders simply— almost as if he's ordering takeout. At once, the others begin circling each other, growling in such a way that you know immediately that they will carry out Draven's careless order easily.

"Stop!" Oracle orders from behind me. At once everything around us is still.

"Four, now you I wasn't expecting."

"That was your short sightedness. Luckily I don't suffer from that."

"Do you think you can kill me, old friend? You're much younger than I."

"We're still old as dirt," Four says easily, stopping only when he's standing beside me.

"The others are minding you like trained puppets. Did you take a page out of my playbook, Four?"

"My name is Oracle now, but I did. I had to, to protect them. They were too vulnerable. I knew they would have your blood in their system, but as they've been unknowingly feeding on mine every day for the last five years, mine is stronger."

"Even the dogs?"

"I had to get creative at times, even putting them to sleep to inject it, but yes, even them."

"They won't like you for that," Draven warns.

"Most likely, but they'll live and you will die and that's an outcome I can live with."

"You forgot one thing," Draven tells him.

"What's that?"

"A gun might not kill you, but it will weaken you so that I can. Five, now," he orders, forcefully. My gaze moves to Five, who is pointing the gun at Oracle now.

"I didn't like your tainted blood, Oracle. Did you really think I wouldn't smell it? We're practically the same age. I'm never going to follow any of your commands," Five laughs. "This will only hurt a little, what comes next will hurt a hell of a lot more, I can promise you."

"No!" Ettie screams and then, before I realize what she's going to do, or stop her, she lunges at Five, grabbing the gun and trying to knock it out of the way before it discharges. "Ettie!" I cry, just as Four orders the others to attack Draven and Five.

It all plays out in slow motion, but as the others advance and

I reach Ettie, the gun discharges, only it doesn't hit Four, or even me.

The bullet rips through Ettie, the smell of her blood heavy in the air. She cries out, falling backwards as I swoop her up in my arms.

44

Leo

The next twenty minutes are a blur. There's fighting all around me, but all I can do is hold Ettie and shove my jacket against her stomach where she's bleeding.

"Hold on, Ettie, hold on."

I keep repeating that, but she doesn't respond and her eyes don't open. Her pulse is weak and heart beat is erratic. I can hear it echoing in my brain. Sirens begin to wail in the background and I hear a scream. I look up to see Eight, now a wolf, jumping off his hind legs and lunging at Draven. His claws sink into the man's chest and he goes down to the ground. Eight bites into Draven's neck, ripping out his jugular and spitting it out beside his body. Five sees the flashing lights of the ambulance and cop cars and pushes Ten to the ground, running away. Four chases after him and I let them go. I can do nothing but hold onto my Ettie and pray a miracle happens.

"Get that ambulance over here," Seven growls out, as we're swarmed by the law.

I leave everyone to deal with the chaos, as I help them put Ettie on a gurney.

"Fuck, is that wolves?" I hear one of the cops say. I look up to see Six and Eight running through a yard and into the timberline. "What in the hell happened here?"

Seven and Ten start talking to them, but by that time, I'm standing at the back of the ambulance as they load Ettie up.

"I'm sorry, you can't ride in here with us," the paramedic says when I start to get in.

"I'm not leaving her," I tell him and I push my way in, not giving them a choice.

"Forget it. Let him ride, this woman is dying," the other guy says when the first one begins arguing with me. I help him close the door and we take off. I watch in silence as they hook Ettie up to oxygen and inject medicine into her. She looks so fucking pale. I close my eyes as they hook her up to the machine and I hear her heart beating erratically.

The ride to the hospital seems like the longest in my life and I can do nothing but will Ettie to hold on.

When we get to the emergency room, I'm following as they wheel her in. The paramedics start calling out to the doctor Ettie's vitals.

"Who are you?" the doctor asks me, my eyes burning, as tears fall from my eyes.

"I'm her ma—her husband. I'm her husband."

"You need to go to admissions and check her in and sign the forms. We're going to need, in writing, that we have permission to operate and her medical history."

"I—"

I stop talking because she's already gone. I stand there until the doors slam shut and Ettie is out of my sight.

"Let's go, Leo. Let's get Ettie registered." I look up to see Ten standing beside me. I know I'm crying. I don't give a damn. I nod, feeling as if my soul is being torn from my body.

"Hold on, Ettie. Please hold on for me."

I urge her and son of a bitch, nothing has ever hurt more than the silence I feel coming from her.

"What's happening?"

Oracle walks in, Seven and Ten with him. I'm sitting by Ettie's bedside, holding her hand and cursing the sounds of the machines that are keeping her alive, grateful and hating them at the same time.

"She's…" I stop unable to get the words out. Just admitting them destroys me. "She's dying."

"They got the bullet out, right?" Ten asks.

"Her blood isn't clotting. They keep pumping new blood in and giving her medicine to help, but she's…she's not responding," I tell them, my voice hoarse with tears that I'm still shedding silently. Each one feeling as if it is burning me. I look down at her delicate hand, wishing I could go back and change things. I should have never let her go out tonight. I knew in my heart that it was going to end badly.

"Do you not listen to me when I talk, Leo?" Oracle asks.

"I'm not up for anymore lessons tonight, Oracle."

"That's too bad. We have two choices here and you need to decide which route we're going."

"Two choices?"

"Either you give Ettie your blood or I give her mine, but it needs to be done now."

"Do you see her? She's got tubes everywhere, Oracle. There's no way she could swallow blood, even if she wanted. Besides, she's only alive by machines. What good could the blood bond possibly do now?"

"I'm going to start holding a damn class once a week for you all."

"Should be a small class, since there's no sign of Jacob or Endy," Seven mutters.

"One problem at a time. The others are safe for now, I can still feel them," Oracle responds. "Ettie is the one we need to save. Draven was an evil bastard, but he was right, Leo. There is power in the blood. We get your blood into Ettie and it will fight to heal her and help her survive."

For the first time in what seems like forever, I begin to feel hope.

"How do we get her to drink it?" I ask, praying he has an answer.

Oracle frowns, walking around to the other side of Ettie's hospital bed. He takes in all the wires, tubes and machines. I can see him quickly calculating and ascertaining what they do. I want to rush him, but I don't. I force myself to wait.

"I'll be right back," he growls and then he's gone. I feel that hope I felt a few minutes ago begin to fade.

"He'll find a way to save her, Leo," Seven says and I want to believe he's telling me the truth, but all I can feel is misery as I look down at the mostly lifeless body of the woman I love more than anything in the world.

A few minutes later, Oracle comes walking back in. He closes the door and looks at Ten. "Stand at the door and don't let anyone in." Ten nods and then he strides over to the bed. "Bring your chair over here, Leo." I do and he waves at me, indicating I need to sit down.

"What are you doing?" I growl, when he unhooks Ettie's IV.

"Saving your mate's life," he says quietly. Then, I watch as he rigs up a tube into her IV and then works with me. Before I can even guess what he's doing, he starts taking blood from my arm, hitting the vein like he's done it his entire life. Then again, for my kind, it's not hard to find the veins which have the most blood coursing through them. Somehow he's made a home-made apparatus that allows my blood to flow into her body. I close my eyes, praying this works.

"How much will it take?"

"I'm not sure. But, we'll use all we can, until we have to stop."

"Don't stop," I tell him. "Give her all she needs. I don't care."

"It could kill you, Leo," he warns.

"Just do it, Oracle. Ettie is all that matters."

I watch Ettie and I'm praying it's not my imagination that her color seems better. Her heart rate seems to get stronger and steadier, too.

"Please, Sunshine. Come back to me."

I beg the words, even as I'm beginning to feel faint. Ettie's beautiful face begins to blur and I know I'm passing out. Just before I lose consciousness, I think I see Ettie's eyes open. Joy surges through me.

"Please be okay, Ettie. Please be okay."

```
┌─────────────────────────────────────────┐
│                                          │
│                   46                     │
│                                          │
│                  Ettie                   │
│                                          │
└─────────────────────────────────────────┘
```

Two Weeks Later

"YOU'RE LOOKING GOOD, ETTIE," Endy says, as he and Jacob walk into my room.

"I'm feeling good," I tell them, smiling. "My only problem is getting an over-protective Leo to let me get out of bed."

"You're still weak," Leo mumbles and I can't help but laugh.

"You do realize you were the one laying around for days after I got home from the hospital, right?" I remind him.

"Just give me this, Ettie," he mutters and I stretch up to kiss him. Our lips touch briefly, but it's enough.

I did heal up quickly. In fact, I was out of the hospital two days after Leo saved my life. I'm recovering, I just have a lot to heal from. Mentally, finding out my mother is dead, bothered me. I cried over her and I wish I understood why. She didn't love me and I can't say I truly loved her and yet... she *was* my mother. Physically, I'm remarkably well, all things considered. Leo's blood helped, but I still had the surgery and the damage the bullet did to my insides to contend with. I truly was close to death. I'm much better now, however, and hopefully I can convince my mate of that tonight. He needs to drink, but has refused until I'm better. Considering how much blood it took to get me fixed up, that means my man is very weak and I refuse to let that continue. We're a team and if what Oracle tells me is true, we'll be a team for a very long time, an eternity really, and I can't wait to spend every moment of it with him.

Stark and Sean come in next and for a minute the atmosphere gets tense. Tonight is a meeting that should have happened a week ago, but I know the guys have been putting it off until I was better.

"So, are we going to talk about the elephant in the room?" Stark asks, never one to shy away from a hard subject.

"You mean your nose?" Leo jokes, though I can tell his voice is strained. He's dreading what comes next, but we both know it has to happen.

Oracle walks in and the atmosphere gets even heavier. Maybe it's because I have Leo's blood now, I'm not sure, but I can literally feel the anger rolling off of the men.

"Am I in time for the party?" he asks, and I notice he's looking very tired. On instinct, I stand up and walk over to him, linking our arms together and putting my hand on his bicep in a show of support, as we face the others.

"You know why we are here," Endy says and on instinct I press my hand harder against Oracle's.

"You and Jacob are leaving," Oracle announces and my gaze cuts to them, willing them to deny it.

But they don't.

"You lied to us," Jacob accuses.

Oracle studies him for a minute, but then shrugs. "I omitted a few things," he allows.

"You knew we didn't need the blood to survive and yet you fed us yours. You lied," Endy growls and it's clear that most of the anger in the room is coming from him.

"I suppose I did, yes. Although, I did do it for your protection. I needed a way to negate Draven's reach on you."

"We should have been told. We all should have been allowed to choose freely," Ten says, letting Oracle know that it's not just the shifters who are unhappy.

"And if you had chosen wrong, some would have died. I did what I did to protect the collective and given the choice…" Oracle moves his shoulders in an indecisive manner. "I would have chosen the same line of action."

"You mean you would lie to us again," Stark questions him.

"If doing so meant saving you? Then yes. Guilty as charged."

"Sean and I can't stay here. Having viewed Scar and Draven up close, and knowing that we were lied to by one of your kind, one we thought we could trust—"

"One of our kind?" Leo questions. "What are you saying, Endy? Did you forget that we were all created the same way?"

"I'm forgetting nothing, but you have an animal inside of you that is dark. You twist things to suit your wants and think that's fine. None of you think anything about forcing something on us that goes against our nature. It's clear we can't live among you," Endy declares.

"An animal inside of us? That's rich. Tell me, Endy, do you have fleas from rolling around in the mountains with the other *animals*?" Stark asks, his voice full of sarcasm.

"You know what I mean. At least our animals are of nature. We're not parasitic creatures that need blood to survive."

"That red gunk in your veins would argue with that fact," Seven returns.

"Actually, it's blue inside of the veins. It only appears red when it reaches air," Oracle supplies helpfully. "While we are bickering there is one very large fact that we all seem to be ignoring," he adds.

"What's that?" I ask, hoping to change the topic before Endy and Seven can get in a fight.

"Scar is still in the wind. He knows where our compound is and he knows the different ways in and out of it. It's not exactly safe for any of us to stay."

"Shit," Leo mutters and he looks at me. I give him a tight, but hopefully reassuring, smile.

"Are you saying that all of us should leave?" Sean asks.

"It might be safer for you in the long term. Scar is very powerful and from Draven's tale of what happened to Scar's mate, it is clear that he is a few bricks shy of a full load."

"Are you leaving?" Stark asks.

"This has become my home. Luciana and I are happy here. I shall remain."

We're all left frowning, wondering not for the first time, who this Luciana is and why no one but Oracle knows she's around.

"Then, I'm staying," Stark says. "I may not like that you lied, but I can appreciate the fact that my head is still on my shoulders."

"I'm staying, too," Sean agrees. "Besides, if I left, Stark would get himself in trouble. He needs someone looking out for him."

Leo looks at me. Thoughts pass between us that we don't need to put into words.

"Leo and I are staying."

"That's it, then," Jacob says and he and Endy begin to walk away. I let go of Oracle and go to the door to stop them.

"You could still stay. You both are welcome here. We're family."

They turn to look at me, sadness on their faces.

"You're already turning into one of them, Ettie. I can see it in your eyes," Endy says and he seems so sad about the fact that I'm changing that it hurts me. I'm proud of being Leo's. I don't see anything at all to be ashamed of. I can see them being upset about being lied to, but I don't understand why they feel they are so different from Leo and the others.

"Where will you go?" I ask, deciding against asking them to stay again. It's clear that they have their minds made up.

"We're going to claim Castle Mountain and Silver Run as our territories. We ask that you stay out of it. We can stay in touch and if we need to come together for a larger problem, perhaps we can work together. But, your kind aren't allowed in our woods."

I step away from him. *My kind.*

"Our kind. That's rich. But go to your mountains and enjoy rolling around in the dirt, while you look down on us in our homes and call us the animals," Stark snarls.

Endy's face goes tight, but he and Jacob leave without another word.

"I guess that's that," Leo says quietly and I can sense his sadness at the way Endy and Jacob left.

"What's next?" Sean asks.

"We live," Oracle responds, and then leaves the room. I walk into Leo's arms and let him pull me close. When I think about how close I came to dying, Oracle's words sound almost as sweet as my man holding me while whispering into my mind.

"I love you, Ettie."

"I love you, too, Leo."

I close my eyes and breathe in his scent and know that if I live forever and one day, that I will love Leo that entire time and into the next world, whatever it may be.

```
┌─────────────────────────────────────┐
│                                      │
│            Epilogue                  │
│              LEO                     │
│                                      │
└─────────────────────────────────────┘
```

Epilogue
LEO

T*wo Months Later*

I STARE DOWN into the eyes of my wife, feeling her pussy trembling around my cock. She's so close to coming, but I'm toying with her, keeping her from going over that final cliff for as long as I can.

"You're my world, Ettie," I tell her kissing her neck and leaving a lazy trail with my lips to her breasts, as I gently suck on each nipple.

"I know, Leo. I know, because I feel the same exact way about you."

We were married just last week at a small church in Billings. Ettie wore a beautiful white dress and looked like an angel. Oracle, Seven and Ten were there. Ettie sent a message to Endy and Jacob through an email she found on a website representing the new business that they've started. It's an outdoor trail guiding business with kayak and tube rentals offered along the river that falls in their territory.

They didn't reply, but when the wedding started, they came in and sat in the back. After it was over, they hugged Ettie and shook my hand, wishing us the best. It's not much, but it made Ettie feel better and honestly was more than I expected.

"I could stay here all day, Sunshine, just like this."

"But, Leo, I need you to move," she groans, her hips pushing up against me, latching so tightly onto my cock that I can't help but groan as I struggle to control my body, not allowing myself to come—even though I could. Something else has to happen first. Ettie has drank from me since that day in the hospital. It's never much and only happens once a month, sometimes twice. I leave it up to her, but demand it happens monthly, as that's what Oracle said was safe. It has brought us closer and deepened the connection between us. We're still learning everything we can do together through our connection, but as time passes and the bond grows stronger—so does our connection.

I stare into her eyes as I bring my finger to my lip. Her eyes deepen in color. They don't change like mine do, but the longer she goes with my blood in her system, the more they deepen in color—especially when she's aroused. I press my teeth against the pad of my thumb, letting my fang prick it. Blood bubbles up, just a small drop and I place it against her lips. She sucks on my thumb almost instantly, her body shuddering as desire slams through her. I begin moving then, riding her hard and taking us both past the point of no return. Just before she comes, I bite into her neck and I'm rewarded with her moan of pleasure, her body quaking as her orgasm rips through her, and takes me along with her.

"I'm pregnant."

I hear her announce that through our connection as I ride out my climax. When I open my eyes to stare at my wife, I see the tears of happiness that are gathered in hers. Later, I will tell her what a gift she's given me. I'll let her know just how much she means to me and how I couldn't live without her.

For now, all I can do is make her come again. I can't seem to get words out to show how happy she's just made me—how happy she makes me every day. So, I decide to show her with my body and that's exactly what I do.

Epilogue

S ix Months Later

"HEY THERE, SUNSHINE."

I grin as Leo walks into the room, my body coming alive and tingling just from having him close.

"Leo," I murmur, pleasure and happiness rich in my voice. He walks straight to me, picking me up in his arms and making me laugh as he settles us back down on the sofa.

"Is everything okay?" he asks, nuzzling the side of my neck.

"Yeah, Honey. I was just helping Stark fill out an online questionnaire."

"Questionnaire?" Leo asks, his brow furrowed. "What kind of questionnaire? You applying for a job, Seven?"

"When are you going to break down and call me Stark?"

"Probably about the time he stops calling me Ten," Sean replies, flopping down in the chair across from us.

"That would be never," Leo laughs and Stark and Sean both give him dirty looks.

"Where's Oracle?" Sean asks and I sigh.

"He's resting."

"He seems to be doing that more and more lately. I don't think we saw him at all yesterday," Leo murmurs.

"I know. I'm worried. He's so sad since the others left."

The room goes quiet for a minute, partly because of our worry about Oracle and partly because of the silence of Endy and Jacob. We've not heard from them at all, and it's starting to get pretty clear that we won't.

"Would you describe my eyes as devilishly handsome or sparkling with humor, Ettie?" Stark asks me.

"They're deep brown, right?" Sean interrupts. "How about we just say they're full of shit, like the rest of you."

Stark flips him off.

"What kind of form are you filling out?" Leo asks, laughing at Sean's joke.

"It's a dating profile," I murmur with a grin.

"Dating profile? For an online dating site? But why?" Leo asks, disbelief thick in his voice.

"You have your Ettie. I want mine. She's out there somewhere and damn it I'm going to find her."

"Stark wants to be in lovvvvveeee," Sean mocks.

"Fuck that, I just want to get laid," he mutters.

Leo laughs out loud. "I can't deny that's a hell of a lot of fun." I elbow him, but that just seems to make him laugh harder.

"I hate you," Stark mutters.

"I'm starting to dislike you myself," Sean adds.

Leo stands up, gathers me in his arms and starts walking toward the door.

"I can tell when I'm not wanted."

"Leo! What are you doing?" I wrap my arms around his middle and hold on as he carries me away.

"Taking you to our room so I can get laid."

"Bastard!" Stark yells out and this time I laugh with Leo.

"You're horrible, Leo, but I love you."

"Love you, too, Ettie," he murmurs as I kiss on his neck.

Once upon a time, I was about as alone as a woman could be and now?

Now, I have everything.

The End.

Jordan's Early Access

Did you know there are three ways to see all things Jordan Marie, before anyone else?

First and foremost is my reading group. Member will see sneak peeks, early cover reveals, future plans and coming books from beloved series or brand new ones!

If you are on Facebook, it's easy and completely free!

Jordan's Facebook Group

If you live in the U.S. you can **text JORDAN to 797979** and receive a text the day my newest book goes live or if I have a sale.

(Standard Text Messaging Rates may apply)

And finally, you can subscribe to my newsletter!

Click to Subscribe

Social Media Links

Keep up with Jordan and be the first to know about any new releases by following her on any of the links below.

Newsletter Subscription
    Facebook Reading Group
    Facebook Page
    Twitter
    Webpage
    Bookbub
    Instagram
    Youtube

Text Alerts (US Subscribers Only—Standard Text Messaging Rates May Apply):

Text *JORDAN* to 797979 to be the first to know when Jordan has a sale or released a new book.

Also by Jordan Marie

The Eternals

Eleven

Stone Lake Series

Letting You Go

When You Were Mine

Where We Began

Before We Fall

Savage Brothers MC—2nd Generation

Taking Her Down

Savage Brothers MC—Tennessee Chapter

Devil

Diesel

Rory

Savage Brothers MC

Breaking Dragon

Saving Dancer

Loving Nicole

Claiming Crusher

Trusting Bull

Needing Carrie

Devil's Blaze MC

Captured

Craved

Burned

Released

Shafted

Beast

Beauty

Filthy Florida Alphas

Unlawful Seizure

Unjustified Demands

Unwritten Rules

Unlikely Hero

Doing Bad Things

Going Down Hard

In Too Deep

Taking it Slow

Lucas Brothers

The Perfect Stroke

Raging Heart On

Happy Trail

Cocked & Loaded

Knocking Boots

Made in the USA
Middletown, DE
29 November 2020